I AM REON

A CHILDHOOD SAGA

S SUSHEELA

Made with ♥ on the Notion Press Platform
www.notionpress.com

Contents

Contents

Author's Note

Thirty seven years of experience as a Lawyer coupled with that of mediating several Family Court cases, listening to what the children from various backgrounds have and have not spoken to me, and to others, and, watching many children climbing up the stairs of court rooms, moving through the corridors of courts, unknowingly growing older and older towards adulthood alongside the litigation induced me to write this short novel. "I am Reon" is a childhood saga.

I know somewhere, deep within their hearts , many children would be searching for their lost childhood. In between they would be trying to find out where how and because of whom they had to lose it . They would even be asking why did not any one do anything to prevent this.

I don't think we have any answers that may appeal to them .

Every one of us has a child, never to die , within us. That child will not die . That child makes us look at the world in its purest form and search for reasons for a meaningful life. It helps us to infuse meaning into life. That child lurking within every individual is the real force that keeps everyone away from being static even at a very old age. With this living spirit within us we live not in wait for death but being all curious to meet a different tomorrow.

Time is ripe for us to understand that none has the right to adversely affect childhood which is a very precious component of human life. Let us be completely with children and see to it that every child enjoys his or her childhood to the fullest extent.

I look forward to many more hands willing to join me in this common pursuit of human welfare.

Thanks in advance.

S Susheela

Foreword

If COVID was a contemporary pandemic, Adverse Childhood Experiences (ACEs) have been an everlasting epidemic. ACEs are traumatic events that occur in childhood and undermine children's sense of safety, security and attachment. ACEs also include experiences like exclusion and discrimination. These are not only linked to the health problems and mental illnesses of the later life of an individual, but also negatively impact the individual's education and livelihood.

There are two ways in which we can view the human predicament. If a child has experienced adverse circumstances, what does that do to her/his life trajectory? Children have many developmental needs – nurturance, nutrition, love, attachment, opportunity, security, encouragement, to name a few. These needs may not be met with because the parents are too busy with their own lives, or there is parental conflict or one parent has mental illness. A child whose 'love' needs are not met with for any reason, grows up into a person who needs love, craves love, demands love, does not recognize love when it is given, is cynical of love or becomes an excessive giver of love.

The second context is an adult in a life cycle stage where s/he exists in a compromised state of well-being. The question here is – what childhood experiences might have been endured to lead to such a compromised state of being.

This book is a poignant and elegant description of such processes. Starting with a child muddling through parental conflict and the secondary trauma of courtroom drama, the story proceeds to further vicissitudes in the life cycle. Characters with fractured identities weave their way into the narrative and lost souls find each other in future timelines of their respective lives.

The book is a timely and serious reminder of our duty to provide children with the warmth, safety and dignity they require for wholesome growth. Childhood cannot be the battlefield in which two adults fight. How childhood vulnerabilities become pathways to adult conflict is sharply brought alive in the narrative strands of individual characters. This book brings to our notice the myriad epochs where a more understanding and compassionate approach would have changed the lives of the protagonists for the better. We have an obligation to recognize and respond to the critical relationship between child protection and mental health.

Shekhar Seshadri

Former Senior Professor, Department of Child and Adolescent Psychiatry, NIMHANS, Bangalore

February, 2024.

Acknowledgements

I have no words to express my sincere gratitude to Mr.Dr.Shekhar Seshadri, Former Senior Professor and Former Head, Department of Child & Adolescent Psychiatry, Former Dean Behavioral Sciences Division , Former Director NIMHANS, who has written a very meaningful foreword to this book. Foreword by Mr.Dr.Shekhar Seshadri, has not only added value to this book but it also reminds us about our duty towards children.

My sincere thanks to Sri.M.C.Prakash, Former Principal and Associate professor of English, Vidya Vardhaka Sangha First Grade College, Bangalore in helping with editing the language part of this short novel.

My appreciation and heartfelt thanks to Sri.Achyuth Nag for designing the cover page in a meaningful manner.

Sincere thanks to Notion Press for coming forward to help in publishing this short novel.

S SUSHEELA

Disclaimer: The names, characters and the situations and incidents dealt with in this novel are all fictitious. No identification with living or deceased persons is intended and no such identification be inferred in any manner.

1

Chapter - 1

I am Reon. Does my name sound English? It doesn't. In the Indian context you may claim it to be a purely traditional name , where, at times, one's name has to be coined from the names of one's parents or grandparents. You will be surprised to know the origin of my name . Though I don't know about my own origin till this day, I do know something about how my name originated. It is not an English name. How could it be? Being staunchly traditional South Indians, my parents would never give me an English name. There had been an incessant fight between them as in the case of any subject under the Sun, about what my name should be. One would commence with some name and the other would counter it with the genealogy of the other. They never agreed on anything, the issue of my name being no exception. Days and years rolled by there being continued disagreements with no consensus. One fine day, each of them, but not both of them, decided severally that I had to be admitted to school. Even this was not their collective decision, but a mutually exclusive decision. Each of them submitted different names before the Principal of the school I was to be admitted into. A noisy quarrel ensued between them unmindful of the onlookers around. I was the only one unperturbed by their shouts and howls. Five years is a long period when you get used to things around you. I was seriously looking at the butterfly which was tirelessly trying to fly escape from the closed window There was a long queue of people seeking admission and I would have to probably wait for a year if that date was missed. My parents were eager to avoid at any cost the loss of the huge amount they had collectively paid for my admission. The Principal and all others standing in the queue were getting restless. The Principal asked me, ' What do they call you at home?' I repeated "Yey, OOy... HOOOOOY, YEEEEY, Re....y , Orrreeeeeey" imitating my mom and dad's voice and their typical South Indian accent. Everyone there burst out laughing. Someone exclaimed, "A very smart child". Yes, I know for sure, specially now, that one is obliged to be smart when neither of one's parents is bothered but only pretends to be. Now I am convinced of Darwin's theory of 'survival of the fittest'. Trying to contain his rising temper, the Principal asked my parents and noted down my mother's name as "Revathy", and my father's name as "Onkar" and took their signatures on some forms and said, rather declared, "Your name is ' Re-On'. ' Re' from Revathy . Madam , it is You and 'On" from Onkar -Mr.Onkar ..it is from You." With this he called, 'Next'. The next person came in with his kid followed by the next. When asked to send me to school from the next week my parents did not comment. I am still trying to figure out whether they were happy that neither of them lost or won the game. No I don't think so. Both bore with the name coined by the Principal because each of them was happy that the other did not win. I came out of the room following them, and at once remembered the poor butterfly . I went into the Principal's chamber, sneaked amidst many people busy getting their children admitted, climbed over the Principal's table, and before he could say anything, opened the window for the butterfly to fly away. The Principal was shocked. I thanked him and ran back home.

I went to school all alone next week, as my father left assuming that my mother would drop me and my mother thought my father would come back to pick me up and drop me at school, as a result of which confusion neither of them turned up in time for the job. They were shouting at each other over phone. Each claimed it to be the responsibility of the other. And I went alone. The peon let me inside the gate and walked me to my class room. I was surprised when the teacher addressed me and said, 'Reon, come here.' I was looking around unsure of who this Reon was. She touched me and asked, 'Aren't you Reon? Is not Revathy your mother and Onkar your father?' 'YESSSS,' I said. 'Come in. Why are you standing there? Children... Look here! He is Reon, a good friend of yours.' The teacher was marking something in a long book. I got confirmed on that day that Reon was and is my name. And it shall be. I could have got it changed at a later stage of my life, but I did not do so not that it comprised components of both my mom and dad's names, but because someone had sewed up both their mouths for the first time through his creativity. The butterfly got his freedom when Reon took birth. In retrospect, I love my name and am proud to be Reon. My mom always called me Re.. which typically sounded like "Ray", and my father, "On" which always sounded like "Own". I now see that my mom's struggle all through was to see that my father was never present in my life, not even in my name, a mission that my father shared vice versa. They were angry whenever I told somebody my name to be Reon ..sounding as Riyaaan. Mom said, 'Say, "Ray"; that is enough.' Father said, 'Tell "Own" and that would do.' Once my paternal grandmother told me, 'Say "RAYOWN", that would make both of them happy.' Poor lady did not know how seriously my parents fought with each other to obliterate each other's name from my mine.

I used to feel at home with my grandmother. But my mother did not like me getting closer to her. Later in life, I understood what made my mother do so. My mother did not like my father's mother as she did not like my father. She did not like me to get close to my grandmother as she did not like her. She wanted me to keep myself away from everyone connected with my father. The story was no different in my father's side. I have never seen anyone related to my mother enter our home. I have a very vague memory of my mother's sister and her husband whom we had met once at a bus stand.

The dynamics of relationship works strangely in a family. When couple start hating each other , and take it as a mission to eliminate the other from the life of children, who all become targets of hatred no one can guess. The circle of hatred gets increased day by day. Over a period of time there will be two different circles of hatred from each side, one claiming the other to be toxic for the children, without understanding the very fact that children unknowingly live in both circles .

Both the parents do not understand that it is hatred that has started taking control over both the circles , and their children are caught within it.

2

Chapter - 2

My association with butterflies is unique. I don't know when it started. May be when I was too young. One day I was crying loudly for milk. My mom who went in to fill the bottle with milk, found that the bottle had not been cleaned since the previous night. It was smelling bad. She shouted at my father and they began to quarrel. Everything came out in their fight except my milk. I moved out quietly and sat on the stone bench in front of our apartment. I was crying. Butterflies were flying happily around. A butterfly would perch on a flower for a fraction of second and move from there. Another would come and do the same. Suddenly a butterfly came and sat on my cheek. I think it sat there for a longer time. May be a few seconds or more. Then came another one. Then they both flew away. What a wonderful feeling it was. I felt very happy. I reflected at once, 'I am not feeling hungry now.' When I was about to wipe the tears from my cheek, Minni, our neighbour's servant's daughter, rushed there shouting, 'Reon, don't wipe them. Let the tears flow. May be the butterflies will return to lick them. They looked pretty on your cheeks." I let the tears alone as told by Minni. But the butterflies did not return. We both waited.

Minni asked me to cry again and I tried, but could not get tears. 'Oh! So sad. Butterflies like anything that is fresh. They don't like anything that is artificial/stale,' said Minni and went into her house. Since that day, whenever I had tears I would come and sit on the same bench. But the butterflies never came near me. May be all tears are not worth their attention?

Yet another evening I sat on the same stone bench watching the butterflies. Minni came running. 'What are you doing?' She asked me in her usual inquisitive voice. 'I am searching for those two butterflies,' I replied seriously. She joined me in the search but we could not trace them. When I was sitting the next day Minni came running to me and said, "Don't search for those butterflies. They have gone to God. My mom told me that all good beings go to GOD very early like my younger brother. Butterflies live only for one day.' Oh My God!. This was unacceptable to me. Only for one day...only for one day... I cried bitterly. I believed Minni, and Minni always believed her mother. Mini would say anything told by her mother in such an assertive voice that I would accept it as it is. No other butterfly came and sat on my cheek. I was disappointed. I did not eat food or drink milk. My mother shouted at me, 'Rey, you are growing old. You have to eat and drink on your own. Don't wait for me to feed you like a one day baby." That expression, "one day baby" began to disturb me a lot. While I was about to enter the bed room, my mom told me, 'Don't sleep next to me. Sleep in that room from today.' I obeyed her orders. Tried to sleep but could not. I was getting restless. Went back to mom's room. She had tightly covered herself with a double blanket. I slept next to her. There was something disturbing me from within. My mom was fast asleep. I just peeped inside my mom's blanket and was shocked to find my mom sleeping stark naked. It had never happened before. I was afraid. I was shivering. I moved out....ran into Papa's room. Papa, half naked, was startled to see me and shouted at me. He warned me to knock the door before I stepped into his room. Told me that he had got much work to do and asked me to get closeted in my room. I came out of his room terribly afraid ..of what... I did not know. I came out and entered my room. But had palpitations. I could hear my heart beats. Again I went to Papa's room. The room was locked. I peeped through the half closed windows, moving the thick and thin curtains a little. Papa was watching something on the monitor. He was half naked. There were naked men and women on the screen coming closer and closer to each other, engaged in weird acts. I started trembling. I ran out to Minni's house. Told Minni's mother that I was afraid to sleep alone and would sleep in their house. Minni was sound asleep. One of her hands was on her mother's chest. I felt Minni was a very lucky child. The poor lady hugged me fast. Though she was very bony, I felt there was something soft in her touch. There was cosy warmth in her embrace. I sensed the same feel of comfort I had felt when two butterflies had sat on my cheek. Minni's mother covered me with her dusty torn blanket. Patted on my back and told me "Beta,..(Son..) You live in a big bungalow. You are very rich. You can't sleep here. This is a hut. Go and sleep at home. Sleep alone in your room as your mom asked you to. But, I tell you, you will not be alone. You will have a beautiful blanket of butterflies. Whenever you are afraid, whenever you feel lonely, they will cover you, they will be with you till the sun rises. No one can see them. Even you cannot. But you will feel them. Javo beta –Javo. (Go son- go).' I trusted Minni's mother. I had no reason whatsoever to doubt her. We trust someone without even knowing why we do. That is trust. Trust is something that gets manifested on its own. I was excited about the blanket of butterflies. I came back home, closed my eyes and slept. As Minni's mother said, within minutes umpteen butterflies came and covered me. I enjoyed the comfort of the blanket of butterflies. I was no more afraid, no more disturbed. Next morning when I woke up I was very fresh but my mom and Papa were both quite exhausted and dull. They were trying to avoid each other and me too. I went happily to school.

A week after that I saw some people near Minni's hut. I was told Minni's father had left for God's abode. I asked Minni, 'Your father used to beat your mother and would always swear at her. Still how did he go to GOD? Minni replied, 'Yes. But my mother says, he gave me i.e., Minni to my mother, and my brother Raju who is already with God. My other two brothers are also given by my father. Because my father beat my mother, he went to God very late unlike my brother Raju, who was very sweet, like your butterflies.'

ᑭᑭᑭ

3

Chapter - 3

Minni lived in a small hut which was, for me, a real museum with myriad things. There was everything you ask for. And strangely Minni or her mother would get whatever was required from that unorganised museum. I used to wonder how big our house was but there was a perpetual quarrel of mutual blame game between my mom and dad eventually with neither getting what she or he was searching for. They would swear at each other and buy it again only to find the same after a few days. There was seldom such confusion in Minni's house. Everyone knew for sure where the things were. No one threw away each other's possessions. There was respect for each one and each one's belongings. I had seen Minni's mother picking up a broken toy of Minni's from near the gutter outside the hut, and wiping it with the fringe of her sari and placing it over the bundle of clothes with a remark that it was a favourite toy of Minni's brother.

There were two plates in their house. Minni would clean the plate after eating from it and her two brothers would together eat in it. When Minni's father came wobbling and faltering being heavily drunk, Minni's mother would send us both away to play outside. I would hear Minni's father shouting at her mother. Sometimes I heard the sound of beating also. Minni never went inside. But I can now understand what Minni would have been going through. Violence – cruelty of any kind - against anyone is unacceptable to a child. Child resists it in its own way. Words fail to express the intra-personal and inter-personal turmoil a child would be going through when one of its parents is causing pain and agony to the other parent. I could see the turmoil that Minni was going through. I could sense how she was struggling to keep it to herself. Probably she was trained by her mother or the situations themselves to negotiate such situations. One thing I can still remember is the confusion in the mind of Minni as a child to decide to accept what was going on under her very nose even when she did not want to accept it. I have seen Minni's mother coming out, arranging everything so that Minni's father ate his meal and then washing his plates as though nothing had happened. May be Minni's mother was used to abuses, beatings and cruelty at her husband's hands. She had accepted life that way. But one thing I can still remember is that she made it always sure that her children remained out of sight of her husband. Probably he was not even aware how many children he had. I had never seen Minni mentioning anything about her father. All her conversations with me revolved around her mom. Her mom would appear either in the beginning or at the end or in the middle of every sentence uttered by her. I could feel Minni's mother pervading the major portion of Minni's life . Minni had seen a real heroine in her mother. Was it because she endured all the cruelty at the hands of her father? Was it because, in a male dominated society , where man notwithstanding being the weakest in all practical forms , was claiming himself to be the hero of the house? But it was Minni's mother who took charge of running the household and managing everything and everyone around as a woman.

I feel, in retrospect, how insignificant father could become for a child and how a child adapts himself/herself to live with the mother alone. It could have equally been vice versa for another child. I was thinking of my own position, which, I thought, was worse than that of Minni. I don't think I had either of the parents in my life in its true sense. How does one understand whether a child has both the parents or not? It is too difficult to discover. No one bothers to delve deep in to understand what a child has or does not have in her life. A child's life has an opaque glass surrounding it. What is visible may not be there in reality and what is not visible may still be there. Minni lived her life as I did mine about which I have no regrets. I don't think Minni had any regrets either. But the fact is that what we missed was as children unknown to the whole world. What is seemingly there for others may not be there at all for a child. Child's world is an entirely different one. Unfortunately it is a world within the world of adults. That is where the whole problem arises. Child's world is narrowed down by adults. Do they have a right to do so? If so, to what extent?

4

Chapter - 4

Everyone in our class was afraid of Badri. He was considered and noted as the only bad boy of the class. Behind his back every one called him “Bady”. I was told that one day he had struck his step mother with a side stool and once with a big strong club. I also knew that one day she came with her head bandaged and complained to the Principal and when Badri was summoned, he came running from the exercise class with his dumb-bells, hit her again with the dumb-bells in his hand in the very presence of the Principal. My friends told me, ‘Bady will go to jail one day. Be careful about him! Do not mingle with him. You will also be in trouble.’ Whenever he absented himself there was always a gossip that he was taken by the police. But next day he would walk in like a hero. I never saw any remorse on his face any day. He had that heroism in his blood is what I thought. He always did whatever he wished to. One day the Principal asked him why he was very weak in drawing and why he did not practice strokes and shades with patience. Badri reparteed the Principal right in the presence of the drawing teacher that the drawing teacher’s mouth stank and standing beside him was nauseating. He continued further to say that the drawing teacher stank from every part of his body and that is why he had begun to dislike drawing. Principal looked straight into Badri's eyes in approval and ran out closing his nose. For me Badri was not a rowdy but a heroic figure. But I do admit this thought in me was not very palpable until something unusual happened between me and the drawing teacher. Our Drawing teacher gave us homework. He asked us to draw the picture of a "FAMILY" and to write the names of the members of the family. Asked us to colour the picture using crayons. I handed over my drawing as did the others. The drawing teacher was in for a surprise. 'What are these... ?' he asked me. "BUTTERFLIES," I said. 'What is this that you have written?' He asked further. 'They are the names of the butterflies,' I replied. 'B1 and B2 are the ones that sat on my cheek. B3 is the one which I moved out from the Principal's room and the rest ..B4 to B6 are from our garden.' 'Who is this? Me-Reon-Who is this?' 'Minni!' 'This lady..?' 'Minni's mom.' 'Where is your father?' 'Father?' I said, 'I drew the picture of my Family!'. The drawing teacher took me to the Principal's chamber. He declared that I was insane and that I should be referred to a psychiatrist. I saw the drawing teacher and the other teachers involved in some deep discussion with the Principal. In an hour's time my mother and father came one after the other. The drawing I drew was shown to them. They sent me back to the class room. I was later told that my parents had a lengthy talk with the principal. Evening when I came back home, I sat on the bench waiting for Minni. She did not come that day, the next day and even the day after that.. she did not come. I went to her house. I was shocked that her house itself was not there. I asked the children of other workers there .."Where is Minni?" They said, 'Don't quote us ..but ...there were complaints against them by your mother and others ..so their house was razed to the ground and they have been shifted to another village.' I had nothing to say. Like a butterfly she flew away.. . I thought for a moment .."Minni is sooooo good, God would have called her too". Now I understand that my father and mother expected their only son to love them... No issues..But did they have any right to prevent me from loving someone else? They always considered me as a member of their family. But I never felt that they were the members of my family. There was a gap, too huge for any bridge to help.

I started hating drawing. But for my drawing I would not have lost Minni. The feeling of deep rooted guilt that how much agony I inflicted on to Minni and her Mom's life just because of my drawing was biting me from within. I decided to give up drawing.

I was telling you about Badri. In our free period called, " relaxation period " I saw Sandeep chasing the butterflies, catching a couple of them in his hands and squeezing them and plucking out their wings. I could not restrain myself. 'Sandeep,' I pleaded with him, 'don't do that.' I shouted at him. He did not stop. Sandeep was a boy who secured the first rank in our class. I complained to the teacher. She said, 'Don't worry about the butterflies, they live only for 24 hours or a little more, may be, for a week utmost. There are better things to do in this world'. I was shocked. I could not digest the fact that a teacher could be so insensitive. When I caught hold of Sandeep's hand, Sandeep hit me hard and I screamed. Suddenly, Badri came from nowhere. He separated us. Sandeep said,

"These butterflies do not belong to him. I will do whatever I wish to with them." I said, "Neither do they belong to Sandeep". Badri gave a strict warning, "Sandeep, walk out.. Don't ever touch a butterfly in your life." 'Are you supporting Reon because he is RICH?.. You should support me, instead. I am a first rank student of the School, don't forget that,' Sandeep said. Badri said in a very soft but assertive tone, "I am supporting Reon because he is saving the butterflies. I will kill you now because you are killing the butterflies." Next minute Sandeep was not seen there. I could see the power of a soft voice for a righteous cause on that day. I said, "Thank you, Buddy," and hugged him. 'You called me Buddy..Buddy...not Bady...?' Badri held me very tight and close to himself. And did not leave me for minutes. I could feel the tears rolling from his eyes. 'Do you know, when you hugged me, for the first time I am getting the same feeling as I would get when my mom used to hug me.' He loosened himself, wiped his tears and walked in the same heroic style. He returned to warn me, ' Look ! Don't ever tell anyone that I cried. If you do, then you will get one GOOSA (big hit) from me and you will be closed. But remember... I will repay you one day or other what you gave me today. If you lose something or someone very special and dear to you, I will be the one to get you back that thing or that person. I have very sweet memories of my mother. My mom always used to tell me, "kisi ke run mein nahin rehana beta..! (Don't be under anybody's debt at any point of time.) I will repay it. Take it from me. It is a promise.' I could not understand ..what was there in my bony body's hug which made Badri remember his mother who was also with GOD? Is human touch so precious? What makes it so special? I was confused in the deep corner of my heart that I was also selfish. "May be, Badri would help me get back Minni!!" If he could not do it who else could?

ÞÞÞ

5

Chapter - 5

Mom came shouting into my room. All my books were scattered here and there. I was trying to make a collage of dry leaves, which I had thoughtfully collected, dried and preserved carefully over several months. Each leaf was chosen with a purpose. I had worked a lot as to where I should paste or place which leaf. 'Shhhhh. What is this nonsense. You are making the house dirty. You have all dirty habits of your father. You are your Papa's son. Stooping too low, running behind people below our status, picking up things like ragpickers... . I am dying here as a single parent and you are.... in your own world!!.' Mom's treasure island opened as usual. I just looked at mom. She asked me, 'Have you ever noticed your father has not been coming home for three months? And it is I...., your mom, who have been struggling hard to bring you up..?' Honestly speaking that was a news for me. I had not noticed it even. ' Re....Do you miss your Papa..? Tell me!! Tell me!! Why don't you speak? Speak...Speak.' She virtually screamed. I said 'NO'. That 'No' gave her a big relief. "Ohhhhhh.. I am relaxed now.' She calmed down a little. It is very strange to notice people feeling happy when they hear what they want to hear from another about the other person whom they have hundreds of reasons to hate. Mom warned me, 'Be careful. Never be your papa's son.' I had no guts to ask my mother, "Who else's son could I be?" She did not wait for my answer either. Next day Papa came to my school. A peon came to my class room with a slip. Our History Teacher read it and announced, ' Reon, your father wants to meet you. Go.' I felt very embarrassed but was left with no options. I followed the peon. Papa took me into his big car where we sat. "Reon, I'm sure you are missing me. But it is not my fault. It is all your mom's... I don't want you to be your mom's son at any cost ...,' he went on talking ...talking...and talking. Did not even wait to check whether I was listening to him or was even interested in listening to him. I was in my own world. I was worried as to what I would tell my friends if they asked me, 'Why had your father come?' I was trying how I would frame a single line answer from all that papa said. After close to an hour, he said, 'Come, let us go'. He left me in the Principal's room. I heard my papa telling him, "Thank you, Sir. Reon felt so happy talking to me at length!!". I cast a strange look at my father. I was much surprised to know that, all that my father wanted was to vomit and vomit and nothing more. That too in front of a child. He did not even have the sense to comprehend what he was doing and why? He did not even understand at the end who had a lengthy talk with whom? I could not recollect a single word that I spoke to my father, because not even a single word had he allowed me to speak. Even to this day I do not know as to why my father came to school on that day and took me out during the class hours. I returned to my class room. In our lunch break, Sandeep came and asked me " What is the news?" There were others behind him. Presently Badri showed himself up and shouted at them, " Chal hut.. (Go! Get away..!!)" All dispersed. I told him what all happened since the previous day. Laying his hand on my shoulder Badri said, 'Reon, it is just the beginning. Both your parents do not want you to be the other's son. It is their fight. Don't worry about it. It is not worth your time. Be happy and be flying like a butterfly, as long as you can.' I recollected. Papa had said many a time, 'You are your mom's son.' And mom had repeatedly remarked, 'You're your Papa's son'. Neither wanted me to be the other's son. There was something missing in it that I caught. Neither ever said, 'You are my son,' let alone saying, 'You are our son!!' Badri was right. I decided. It is not worth brooding over the fight between the parents who consider their child as their individual personal and absolute property.

6

Chapter - 6

I was writing something during my lunch hour. Suddenly the peon came and took me to the office room. This time it was my mom. The Principal said, ‘ Go with your mom to court, the Judge wants to speak to you.’ My mom added, ‘Tell him Sir. Tell him to behave himself and not to bring disgrace to your Institution. ’My mom dragged me with her. She was advising me nonstop on what I should tell the Judge about her and Papa. The crux was only this, everything good about her and all bad about Papa. It was my first visit to the court. As we entered the court complex, I was thrilled to see so many people moving –running-dashing-sitting-standing-sleeping-scolding-fighting- praying. I understood that the court is nothing but a miniature world, a micro-world. My mom's lawyer came and said ‘Hello’ to me. I reciprocated the greeting. Another lawyer came and said, ‘Hi! Smart boy.’ I waved my hands. My mom pinched me. ‘He is your Papa's lawyer. You should not have wished him’. I said I liked his clean glasses. My mom's lawyer removed his dirty glasses and wiped them with the edge of his shirt. I was sitting next to my mom. My father was sitting on the other side. He was asking me to come and sit next to him. My mother was holding me fast so that I could not go. She did not even know that I had no intention to go. As the Judge came, my Papa's lawyer said something. The Judge asked me to go and sit next to my Papa. My mother hugged me ..cried and asked me to go to my papa. She felt as though I was permanently moving away from her. If I am right, it was for the first time, I remember my mom hugging me. It was just a contact of two bodies. There was nothing much to it. I don't think I can even call it a hug. How human touch can mean nothing was understood by me on that day. I went towards my father. He moved from his chair. Hugged me, held me tight to his body. It was the first time he was doing that I his life. I felt suffocated. I noticed how uncomfortable somebody's hug could be, even if that some body is your own mother or father.

I was lost in my own world looking at my shoes. But I was thinking of Minni, her mother's hugs, the butterflies and Badri. Suddenly I heard someone shouting, 'REON !!REON!!'. I stood up! The Judged asked me to come nearer. I obeyed. 'What are you doing? You should be attentive. It is your case. Don't you know?' I just blinked. She asked my name, my principal's name, the name of our school etc.. and introduced my mom's and papa's lawyers. I did not wish either of them. I was looking around in search of someone. The Judge asked me, 'What are you looking for? It is your case.' I said, "Where is my Lawyer?" The Judge was stunned. 'Your Lawyer? What are you asking for?' I asked her, ' You said it is my case, so I was looking for my lawyer. Thought he /she would come.' The Judge and the entire court hall turned suddenly silent. The Bench Clerk said, 'You should not put questions to the Judge.' I bowed as was taught by my Principal. The Judge asked the Bench clerk to get me into her Chambers. She gave me biscuits. She asked me in a very polite voice, 'Reon, your mom wants you to continue in the same school and wants your father to pay the fees, you father wants you to study in a different school. Where do you want to study?' I said, 'Anywhere'. ' Anywhere that can stop my mom and Papa fighting over the choice of my school.' 'What is your choice?' The Judge asked leaning towards me. I said, 'Anywhere I can stand out of their fights. Move away....'. She leaned back on her chair. Closed her eyes. I started enjoying the fish in the aquarium. Suddenly I saw that there were tears rolling down from the eyes of the Judge. I went near her and wiped them slowly. She hugged me. She kissed me. I wanted myself to be the butterflies' blanket covering the Judge. I wanted to give her that comfort. I don't know how she felt. Within minutes she controlled herself. Called the Bench clerk and asked him to take me out. I came back and sat next to my father. The Judge came..wrote something ..and read out something. My mother took me back with her. She thanked me, 'You saved my face Re ... I was sure you would have said everything good about me, and was sure you would have shown your father's other face, his true face to Madam Judge.' She never asked me as to what I spoke ..in those 3-4 minutes' time with the Judge. She imagined all possible things I could have said good about her and against Papa. That evening, Papa rang me up. When I said, 'Hello,' he said, ' Ow..n. You cheated me..exactly like your mother. You proved that you are your mom's child.' He disconnected the phone. Till this day I don't know what the Judge wrote or read.. No one showed it to me. None asked me to tell about the conversation or the dialogue that went on between me and the Judge in her chambers.

Now I know...Alas! When it comes to a child ..it is the human imagination rather than reality that holds the reins.

The child has 'no say' in anything. I feel, the child's life is just like that of a butterfly.. very short... . May be that is why no one is serious about it. No one understands that a child will not be a child for ever . The child will become a man or woman or.... How cruel the world can be to segregate childhood itself which is an integral part of life as though it has no individual existence? I now recollect what Antonie de Saint-Exupery said in The Little Prince.." All grown-ups were once children....but only a few remember it."

7

Chapter - 7

Reading is my passion. Spending time with books is really amazing. I spent my time in conversing with each of the characters in every book that I read. I wanted to know more and more about each character. My thought process always revolved around, 'Why he or she did what she did or why he or she did not do what he/ she could have done.' Half the books in our school's library were regularly being taken by me and read. Every teacher was surprised. 'Do you just take them home, or do you really read them?' was the usual question asked by them. They would cross check, asking me to tell something about some character in the book. I would start and after a minute or two they would stop me. They never wanted to listen to me. They just wanted to test whether I had read those books or not. People are so busy. They do find time to talk, just for the sake of talking, but they do not find time to listen. I was wondering if everyone keeps on talking without listening, where will the words go. Won't the space get crowded with sound and noise? Won't there be a collision of words? One may feel hurt to know the intentions of others. It is ideal not to bother about them, as one does not have any control over them.

I slowly began to understand that the world is huge ...very huge ...so huge that when we are not comfortable somewhere ..we always have another place to move to. When the school bell rang, I would see a different glow on the faces of hundreds of students of our school. May be because they were going back 'HOME'. When I asked a few friends, they said, ' Are yaar...ghar tho ghar hotaa hai! Uskaa majaaa hee alag hai.' (Dude, home is a home, it's a different kick altogether'). I tried to get a taste of it..but failed. Who makes a home? Mother? Father? Children? Or all together? These questions started bugging me. I consoled myself. When we have such a beautiful home in the "world" for us, why do we need another smaller home? Strange. A child always gets an answer to its questions that would comfort him because there is no one who can take time to answer a child's questions. Every child finds answers to all its questions on its own.

I was telling you about my association with books. My mother never wanted me to be put to a boarding school. She thought, if I went to a boarding school, everyone would think she was an irresponsible mother who kept herself busy outside always, without bothering about the one and the only child. My father always declared that he would not pay my fees if I was put in a boarding school. He justified it by telling everyone, 'If children study in ordinary schools, they will be aware the ups and downs of life very well.' But I still remember his wild and violent reaction when I asked him whether I could go to the government school where Minni went. Is school meant to be something that would give relief to parents? Are schools being respected because they share the responsibilities of parents? I am yet to find an answer to these questions. Whatever it is, my school did not permit the students to be there after 5 PM. I was compelled to get back home. Who was there for me..? Milk in the flask..biscuits in the jar.. a note on the dining table...what I should not be doing...and what I should be doing..and how..? “Instructions and Instructions”. Just because we are children, should we have to live always on the instructions of others? How unfair! We are not even allowed to make our requests let alone giving instructions. Damn it! Let me go to books... That is how I always moved closer to books. ‘Why do you spend your time with non-living things..shhhh...objects... like books?’ My mom shouted at me many a time. I wanted to ask her who are the living persons at home but I never did. Children do not ask questions till they reach a certain age. Not because they don’t have questions. But they know very well that their parents cannot answer their questions. Their parents cannot even comprehend their questions. Who will try to understand that children may be heavily loaded with several un-answered questions? Some questions keep haunting them even after they have grown into adults or even when they have grown very old. I had only two options. Keep reading books so that questions did not bother me or read books so that I get answers to my questions from them. For me books were never non-living. They were not ‘shhh..objects’!. They were not as short lived as butterflies either. I was surprised by the fact that some books have lived through ages..but the butterflies died very soon. I loved both.

ϸϸϸ

8

Chapter - 8

Court hearings were very common. If parents have a case, their child automatically knows more about the court and the related issues than the parents or their lawyers. I could get to know when there was a court hearing even 2-3 days before the actual date of hearing. My mom's soliloquies would be longer and longer. 'I did this for you...that for you... your father did not do this or that.. I am a single parent striving hard. You father is enjoying life with "xxxxx"s . If you were not born I could also have been a free bird. Your father insisted that I should give birth to a son for his Khandan /dynasty to continue its name. Now! Your father is out ...out somewhere --- sleeping with someone ...shhhhh!. Dirty fellow.' The day before the hearing milk would spill on the table, the dustbin would be kicked..the maid-servant would be shouted at for no fault of hers... Mom would struggle hard to take her big car out from the garage which otherwise she would do effortlessly. I would not even utter a single word in those three or four days. After the hearing? It all depended on what happened in the court. At times she would be flying. "Oh! That Judge! Wonderful. When your father's lawyer asked for adjournment again, he gave him back nicely... "Another day my mom would say, "The case got just adjourned.. The Judge said, "No time for this case today". Next time I will try to sensitize the Judge to the problem I am facing as a woman . The judges should be gender-sensitive.' When something, according to her, did not go to her taste there was hell at home after the hearing. Milk and snacks were not kept on the table. 'I am out of mood. Manage yourself,' was a regular note on the dining table. Over a period of time, I noticed, my mother did not even place the written note on time. She kept it back in her purse, and placed it on the table either much before or after the court hearings. I could sense that my mom was losing her calm and focus in many aspects of her life .I was not that important for her amongst many other haunting issues. I accepted it as part of the court proceedings. For some court proceedings are similar to going through a terminal illness. My mom was one such. Badri asked me once, 'Why do you keep yourself so silent? Why don't you speak like all of us? Are you like this at home also?' I just smiled and kept quiet. I can count and tell you. I would have spoken 4-5 sentences and 10-20 words in a month with my mom and only over phone with my father.... oh! That was a big mess. l received several notes sent by my father to my Principal telling that I did not pick up the call on the land line on such and such a date at such and such a time, as per court directions. Every time the Principal called me and showed the same to me, I would say, 'I did not receive any communication from the court.' I did not want to say my mother did not inform me at all. I knew my mother did not want me to talk to my father. She let me speak only when the court warned her of serious action. She would stand behind the curtain in front of me and give umpteen instructions through gestures. The moment I said, 'hello', my father would ask, 'Is your mother around? Tell me the truth.'And, without even waiting for my answer, he would rattle out his soliloquy... how much he loved me..and how much my mother hated me ..and why I should get back to him. After 10-15 minutes, my mother would come and snatch the phone and shout at my father, "Your time is over. Don't violate court orders by talking for more than 15 minutes." All that I would have spoken would be hardly 3-4 words. It never ended there. She would enquire, 'I heard you say, "YES". For what did you say, "Yes"? Did you agree to go with him and stay with him, and not to see my face till you die? I heard you say "never". What was it for?' MY GOD! It was an ordeal for me. On the days when my mother had her official duty it was different. She would instruct our maid to monitor the time. Poor lady, she had to bear with three days' boring lectures by my mother for a ten minute phone call. That lady would be waiting behind me. My mother's interrogations stopped gradually. I was always wondering why mother stopped asking me about the details of our conversations. Later I came to know that my mother was getting our conversations recorded. I failed to understand what she could do by eavesdropping on the conversation between two individuals? She failed to understand that she had no control over either my father or over me. She failed to understand that it was she who had moved the court for divorce, and yet she wanted to control him? Of course both were always competing with each other in controlling me . My father would always ask me, 'Why don't you speak to me wholeheartedly? Is that 'xxxxx' controlling you? Don't be afraid. I am with you.' "Papa..have you ever allowed me to speak"? I wanted to ask him, but never did. I am still unable to understand why people spend so much of their energy in struggling to control the words, feelings, emotions, acts and behaviour of others, over which they don't have any control? Why don't they work on themselves? Aren't court proceedings an ordeal for children? Some questions are meant to remain as questions only. They never have answers. But a strange part of questions is also that some children grow more with questions than with answers.

9

Chapter - 9

I started loving court hearings when my parents' case moved to a higher court. There was a big waiting lounge for children. There were small balls, toys, pictures of vegetables , fruits and animals with the alphabet pasted on the wall, a small slide a cricket bat and ball set etc., There were story books too.... Some one thought that children should not be waiting in the court room but they could wait here. Some how I felt that I lost the opportunity of enjoying the kick that I used to get by being in the court hall. I was supposed to be in the waiting lounge to spend two hours with my father between 3 PM and 5 PM every week. Never did my mom get me there on time . My Dad used to be there on time. The first half an hour would be diligently spent by both of them on a fight as to why I was not brought there on time. When the screaming and shouting against each other would get a little high, the Centre Head would give a big sermon to both including me. Every time he would say something to them, he would look at me and say, "Did you understand? Be careful!." At the end, he would ask me, "What do you say?' I would reply, "My mom need not bring me every time, I will myself come and report." The

Centre Head reported something in writing and that was it. I never failed to be there on time. I loved to go there on time going by the clock. While I was always on time, strangely my dad stopped coming there on time. He would come late at times by half an hour and at times when half an hour was left for the scheduled meeting to end. During the first few days he began to give a lengthy explanation on why he got late.. later he stopped it too. He would give me sweets, books, dress etc., and ask me to play with someone there or play on mobile games. He would also sit there doing something on his mobile. "Candy Crush"!! He asked me once why I did not play that. He said it would take me out of my depression. Was I depressed? I did not say anything. I simply said I would love to read books and chose something to read. There were hardly 3-4 sentences that would be spoken in the air between us. What the hell this, strongly fought or contested issue of "visit" meant to my father I never understood. Slowly I started realizing both my parents were fighting against each other "THROUGH" me but not "FOR" me.. To whom could I tell this..? To my mom's lawyer? Dad's Lawyer? Judge? Centre head ? I did not dare do it. Not because I did not have the courage. But I knew for sure that each of them would say," You are a child..you stand out of all these." It is unfortunate that the entire court case that was moving around me.. was going on very much without me consulting me. Once I heard the Judge telling some other party, "If need be, once we will talk to the child". I wanted to ask, "Why once?" Every hearing should be a hearing with the child. "If need be, the Judge can talk to each of the parents once." I loved my dad's lawyer for some reason. There was always a nice smile of understanding. He would wish me eluding my mother's eyes. One day

I caught hold of him in the waiting hall. I asked him, "When will they allow me to speak?" He looked at me for a few seconds, took a long breath and said, " When you grow big!" He saw the disappointment in my eyes. Why should every one expect a child to grow ... to grow ..to grow...? Is it because once the child becomes an adult their responsibility is not there any longer? I thought it is an attack on the childhood. "Sabotage"? Strong words began to pop up in my mind. I restrained myself. I thought I should not corrupt my mind. I should allow myself to feel the uncomfortable heaviness. I should be like a butterfly.. be light..very light.. keep flying.. over all plants...looking at different flowers...perch on some flower for a second or two and move away...move away ..faaaar...very faar!

10

Chapter - 10

Suddenly there was a change. My mom informed rather notified me one morning that as per court orders I should meet a psychologist, and my mom and dad would not be allowed inside the room. I did not ask her why. I was accustomed to taking life as it comes. In a way a court fight between parents moulds a child differently. If I asked any question, I would not get any answer but my mother would talk ..talk...and talk about how bad my dad was.... Of course I was given permission by the court to speak to my father at any time..(as told by my father). I knew if I asked my father why I should meet a psychologist, the result would be no different. He would enumerate everything under the sun against my mom. Who will answer a child's doubts? Parents..? If not, who else? Who will understand them as they are...? Parents...? If they fail who else will have to..? Sorry the words "will have to" is too much taxing. I know. But everyone forgets the fundamental truth that every child wants to be understood. It is unfortunate that a child will not have any one even to approach irrespective of whether he/she would be understood by that other person. Two more days were left.. . Badri was my saviour. I asked him.

Hats off to him and his boldness.. Badri started .."Arrrey –arreyy. Chodo yaar (Leave it Dude!!). Don't be afraid.. no one will be as bad as the persons whom you already know." I know, for sure , he meant ..and obviously meant those persons I know to be my parents. He continued, 'Meet that psychologist. Don't be afraid. A psychologist is only a writing doctor. I have met one once, when I had given a big goosaa to my father's that lady.."XX"! He asked me so many things..about food, about my hair style..about my teachers.. neighbours . He showed me some nice pictures also... He asked me why I spoke so loudly..? and...and... he asked me who is my good friend.. He was jotting down continuously while I was talking to him . I did not tell your name.. because tomorrow he should not write that I was influenced by you to hit that lady "xx""! I said ...I don't have any friends. But Yaaarrrr... (dude..) you are my best friend. Sorry that I told a lie to the psychologist. But I know, you will not tell a lie.. If the psychologist asks you.. tell the truth , as you do always... tell him whoever is your good friend.. But don't mention that goonda Sandeep's name. " I was completely relaxed. How talking to another human being and sharing one's fears helps one is something to be experienced, it cannot be explained in words. I started looking forward to meeting the psychologist. I was more than excited. Some people make things and situations about which we have imaginary fear very much acceptable. Badri was one such in my life.

ÞÞÞ

11

Chapter - 11

I entered the psychologist's room. Well dressed Dr.Susan stood up and walked me near her chair and made me sit on a chair adjusting the levels. I loved the smell of the room which was not smelling like a typical doctor's dispensary. There were no tablets, medicines arranged in the shelves. I could understand Dr.Susan was only a 'writing doctor'. I understood that 'a psychologist is only a writing doctor. She does not give pricks, touch your body...'. Badri was absolutely correct. She was simply talking to me, very sweetly too. She gave me papers and crayons. Asked me to draw the picture of my family. Insisted that my father and mother and my home must be there. And, no outsiders should be there. Either my father or mother or both, I guessed, might have told her as to what I had drawn during my primary school days. I remembered the picture I drew when I was in primary school with butterflies as members of my family. I began to sweat. Dr. Susan was shocked. She came near me and placed her palm on my forehead. 'Reyon, don't draw if it disturbs you.' She said in a low, soothing voice. I recalled what Badri had told me, "But I know , you will not tell a lie.. If the psychologist asks you.. tell the truth , as you always do... ." I felt relaxed in a minute's time and began to smile. The doctor did not understand that Badri was my medicine, be it for my depression or anxiety or anything. I started asking myself, would she, being a psychologist, be aware that "One human being can be a medicine for another human being." "Companionship" is the best medication for child! But how could I tell her all this? I did not want to bring Badri into picture. I wanted to protect him as he had done to me. Luckily Dr.Susan did not ask me, "Who is your best friend?" I drew the picture of a farm house with trees, plants, a hillock.. a river, the sky.. an evening sun and of course some butterflies here and there. Inside my closed house was my MOM. Outside the house I was standing looking at the butterflies. I had drawn a tree at a considerable distance, under which my DAD was standing. I handed the picture to Dr. Susan. She was very happy with my drawing skills. Of course she did not know that I had won many prizes in drawing competitions, but I had stopped working on my skills because of my parents. Many had even told me that one day I would become a great artist. She studied the picture deeply and wrote something at length (a writing doctor!) and asked me to leave the room. Of course, she gave me her number and told me to feel free to contact her if ever I wanted to talk to her. I simply took the card and dropped it in my pocket only to throw it into the dustbin as soon as I came out of the room. Dr. Susan or any other Doctor was not my choice anyways. For me Badri was the only Doctor of my choice.

PPP

12

Chapter - 12

I was asked to be present when the court opened the sealed cover given by Dr. Susan. After reading it, the Judge showed it to both the lawyers and asked for their opinion. My dad's lawyer said, 'The child has drawn the picture of the father standing far away, but father is facing the son. That means the child wants to be with the father and the child is missing the father. Hence the child must be under the father's custody or at least unrestricted visitation rights with overnight custody and half of holidays must be given to the father." Looking at the picture, my mom's lawyer commented, "The child has drawn the father's picture far away from him and his mother. There are hills and rivers in between. That means the child wants to keep himself away from the father. The child does not like the father. Hence no visitation rights can be allowed to the father until the child turns eighteen." The drawing I drew moved from one hand to another... I was surprised. I never knew there could ever be so much of discussion on a child's drawing. The same drawing getting interpreted in multiple ways! Amazing... I had never realised that a child's status of life can also be measured and decided on his/her drawings... . I did not even bother to know what the court ordered and why it ordered so. I had learnt to say "YES" to most of the things in life knowing fully well that telling "no" would cost me more than anyone else in the bargain. I asked the court to give back my drawing The court said, "No, sorry. It is a part of court records." I felt disappointed. Firstly, because what I drew was not returned to me and secondly because, none asked me to explain the drawing that I had drawn.

I explained everything to Badri . I drew a rough sketch of my original drawing and showed it to him. He said in his typical voice, "Fools!! But let me explain to you how I would have interpreted your drawing.. You are away from both father and mother, and you are with nature..and only with nature." I was shocked to know that there could be persons like Badri in the world who would understand you exactly as you want to be understood. They understand you better than your parents. Oh! The world is so beautiful. There is no dearth of persons who can understand you. I was overwhelmed. I broke into crying. I hugged him. He caressed my back gently and hugged me. I felt the comfort of the "butterfly blanket" which was covered over me by Minni's mother. I found that even Badri was crying. But I knew that he never liked someone speak of his tears. Though I wanted to wipe his tears I did not. I kept quiet. I wanted to congratulate him. He was a judge ..He was a psychologist.. He was a good friend. He was my saviour.. He was my lawyer ... He was my doctor. A long silence ensued between us. There are some in the world to understand you, even when you do not speak up. Badri told me once again, "Oh! Whenever you hug me, I get a feeling that my mother is hugging me. But remember Reyon, I will not keep your runn (debt). My mother said, 'Never keep any body's runn (debt). Repay them.' I will repay you when the time comes." He wiped his tears. I pretended as though I did not notice it. I was about to go.. Badri called me in a loud voice, "Ray!! Rayo...n! Come here. I want to ask you something. Whom do you miss always? Don't answer ..if you don't want to." I looked at him and said, "MINNI". I could sense the disappointment in his eyes, because I had not said "You, that is Badri." He said, "Chalo../ Move.... I will get you your MINNI. This is my promise to you." He moved away fast..very fast..as though he was on a mission. He walked fast lest I should notice his deep disappointment.

All said and done, I lost my interest in drawing. I did not want someone to interpret my drawing the way in which I did not want it to be interpreted. I remember getting inside an art museum and listening to an artist who said that as he lays his hand on the canvas, something gets created, and he does not pre-meditate on it. But, I am not like him. If I had been, I would have been recognized as a great artist by today. I never drew anything from that day. When I look back at life I feel that "The artist in me was lost by me in the court hall." May be, I am wrong... May be, I am right....

13

Chapter - 13

Things were going out of limits. Whenever my mother was around, I felt there was less oxygen and felt suffocated. She never accepted me as a child or as an individual. She always saw her husband -my dad- along with me- whenever she spoke to me, or was even looking at me. For her, it was not just Reon, her son.. It was her son and her husband overlapped. Some strange vibes always moved from her, passing through her room to my room reflecting her disturbed feelings. She was never quiet or calm..even when she was silent. The situation with my father was never the better. He was always in a hurry, jumping up and down. His shoulders were jumping up and down whenever he spoke to me. His body was either moving horizontally tilting this way or that way or up and down. I could always hear the sound of his every breath. Why was he so anxious while speaking to me? I could never understand. I could feel that he saw my mother in me and he wanted to see me alone..but was unable to.. even when only I was with him physically and my mother was never around. He always felt and was of course sure that I was tutored by my mother. He reiterated the same in the court. He told the Judge, "My son does not speak to me at all." My mother who was very much there could have said, " He does not speak to me either." I was asked again to meet a psychologist. This time it was not Dr. Susan. It was Dr. Arathi. She asked me, 'With whom do you want to speak?' I said, "Butterflies." 'I am asking about human beings,' she said trying to hide her astonishment. I wanted to say 'Badri'. But something in me asked me to stop. I said, 'I don't like to speak unless it is very necessary.' Thereafter to whatever she asked me, I just looked at her, nodded this way or that way.. did not answer.. or answered with a monosyllabic 'yes' or 'no'. I was asked to go back. Dr. Arathi's report was placed in a sealed cover and sent to the court. Dr. Arathi's report was a single liner . "The boy is normal in all respects." The Judge read and showed it to my mom and dad and both the lawyers. I could see that my dad was disappointed by the report. My mom was happy. Not because the report said, 'I am normal ' but because my dad's accusation that I am not normal, and that this statement indicated that my mom was responsible for my abnormal or not so normal behaviour turned out not to be true. I felt as though I was an ammunition in a war between parents. Why was I being dragged into all these? Just because there was a conflict between my parents, should the child be subjected to evaluation repeatedly, should the child be questioned and cross examined...should the child be advised on dos and don'ts relating to the child's behaviour with either or both the parents? I decided to get out of the mess. I wanted to consult Badri. I knew for sure he would have some answer to my problem.

I went to school in all enthusiasm the next day. Badri was absent. He did not turn up for three more days. On the fourth day our school's aaya (maid) came and handed over a folded piece of paper. She told me in a whisper, 'Badri asked me to give this to you.' I was surprised. Took it from her and came back home. I did not want to read it in the school. I did not want any one to know anything about Badri. Badri's letter is something very special to me. It is still with me.

It read....

My Dearest Ray..

I am running away from my home. I have failed in all tests and internals. My father is thinking of putting me in a boarding school. I don't want to be there. I don't want to give my freedom away to anyone. I don't want to depend on his money. That "XX" of my father will frown. I will earn my living. Don't search for me. I will meet you some day. I will get you your MINNI. I will not break my promise.

Your dearest ..B..

Below his name he had drawn a not so beautiful picture of a boy (marked B) holding another boy (marked R) on his shoulder. Probably it was the only picture he ever drew. I loved it. I loved to be on Badri's safe shoulders. I loved the fact that Badri was carrying me safely. I felt so much comfortable with the fact that I would never be allowed to fall. Badri would never let it happen.

I heaved a deep sigh. I hid the letter in a safe place. I went to sleep. Every time the words in his letter disturbed me and troubled me, the picture would come in front of my eyes. I would feel that Badri was there ... there... . I had not lost him. He was still carrying me. He would continue to carry me.

I know that all may not agree with me that some pictures can give immense comfort to an individual. Was it just a picture? It was much much more than that. It was a strong reassurance that I was not without anyone to look up to. I always opened my box and looked at this picture whenever I was afraid.. disappointed ..or disturbed. What gives strength to one is purely individualistic. I have seen people keeping pictures of God- Christ – Cross- with them, or some holy thread tied around their neck or hand or shoulder. Probably it is only I who have kept the picture drawn by Badri. No one would believe the fact that the picture of Badri carrying me gives me a secure feeling that nothing ever has given. The blanket of butterflies has given me comfort.. Badri's drawing removed the feeling of insecurity troubling within me.

Badri's drawing, Badri's moving away from me.. were not all that easy for me to digest. I was trying to adapt myself to a new situation. In between I was ordered by my mother to attend a program where some experts wanted to interact with children of separated parents, or parents going through the process of separation. Some experts were supposed to come. I went there. I saw many other children of plus or minus my age. Sanny was sitting next to me. She was continuously engaged in reading something. She asked me, "Where is your note sheet?" I was surprised and said, 'I don't have any.' She said, 'You prepare one, at least now . You are with your mother, aren't you? Or with your dad? Your mom /dad did not give you one. Look here, I will show you my sheet.' She thrust the note sheet in my hand. I began to read it ..'I am disappointed by my dad. He hates me ..he hates my mother. He has kicked her in my very presence. I cannot forget it. Whenever I see him, I remember it ..... ' It went on and on. I was not interested in reading it anymore. I stopped in between and gave it back to her and asked her, 'Are you going to tell them all this?'

"Yes! Otherwise my mom will kick me. What about you?"

'You talk to them first. And..., if you start telling them all that is noted down in your sheet, I don't think they will get time to ask me anything.' I told her as though I was asking her to help me out.

'You will be the luckiest then,' Sanny said.

No one understands how troublesome it is for a child to speak to someone against one's father or mother. It is something that can only be experienced by very unfortunate few. Why does a parent influence a child to have his or her opinion reflected by the child as though it is the child's opinion? I always hated people forming opinions. I hated it further more when people thrust their opinions on others. I never liked any one influencing me with opinions notwithstanding the fact that I would have individually agreed with it. Till this day I am unable to understand what an opinion is. Is it just a thought... a feeling.. which may be even a passing thought or feeling? Which may change or found to be incorrect sometime later? What is the basis for the opinion? Is it someone else's opinion? Can decisions forming the life of children be taken based on the opinions of either or both the parents or experts or judges? The entire world is to be available equally for children. It cannot be restricted to some and only some.. adults, their opinions... their disagreements.... Who empowers anyone to think and talk for the children? I am yet to understand this.... Does age curtail an individual's right to live the life to its fullest potential? How does a child live its child's life?

14

Chapter - 14

Things did not go as I had expected.. Someone called my name.. Reon..Reon.. followed by an announcement in the loudspeaker, 'Mrs. Revathi and Mr. Onkar, please get your child to room number 6.'. Sanny pushed me. She was beaming. Her eyes were sparkling only to demonstrate that 'she was right and I was not.' I went inside room number 6. There were five of them- two gents and three ladies. 'Have your parents come?' I said, "No". 'Are they waiting outside?' "No." 'Please sit.'

I was asked to sit in the middle surrounded by five persons- complete strangers to me. Their questions unwound. May be those were common questions to be asked to every child or were completely child-specific ..I did not know. I thought they were surprised by my answers, as after my answer to each of their questions they started looking at one another. 'What do you like?' 'Everything.' 'What do you hate?' 'Nothing.' 'Whom do you love?' I did not answer. 'O.K. Whom do you hate?' 'None.' 'Who is your best friend?' I remembered Minni and Badri. But I did not answer discreetly. 'Don't you have one best friend to play with you?' " NO." 'What do you do if your father tells something against your mother?' "Nothing." 'If your mother does the same?' "Nothing." 'Do you fight with your parents?' "NO." 'In which school do you want to study?' "Any school." 'Do you know why we are asking you these questions?' "NO." 'Do you want to know?' "NO." 'Are you disturbed?' "NO." 'Do you get angry with your parents?' "NO." 'Tell me something about yourself.' I did not answer. They repeated the question .. "I am .... I am, what I am.." I said ..putting a full stop to all their questions. All of them stood up one after the other. I was still sitting. Suddenly someone knocked the door. My father was waiting outside. He rushed in. All at once he said, "My mother is serious and she wants to see Reon, and I want to take Reon with me." My mother came rushing. As usual heated arguments ensued between my mother and father. Mom dug out everything from the past.. My mother was not allowed to attend the cremation of her maasi (aunt), when I was five month-old. Even my mom's massi wanted to see me. But my father had not allowed her to go. So, now, her logic was that I should not pay visit to my father's ailing mother. The five persons who were trained to interact with children tried their best to calm down my parents. At last a formula was arrived at with great difficulty. My father would take me to his mother. Next day he would drop me., and, even if his mother dies, he will not be permitted to take me again and I will not be permitted to go for the funeral. What started as a session for me ended as a session of conciliation for my parents. It is very unfortunate that it is the parents who fight.. who discuss.. who agree..who disagree in the name of the child. All said and done, eventually, I went with my father. I heard one amongst the five experts telling the others, "Look at the boy..he is as he was when he entered the room. There is something special in him." I was anxious for a minute thinking, "What if that something special in me gets translated as something abnormal in me?" Who understands what all unknown fears w haunt a child ? I felt completely helpless. I started shivering. Suddenly I decided to regain my strength. I began to think of butterflies.. I quietened myself. I kept moving with my father. As usual it was my father who was talking non-stop without even bothering to know whether I was listening to him or not. The first few miles he was telling me everything about his mom..how she took care of him.. and others. He was crying as he explained about her terminal illness. In between he ushered in my mom.. and he became very ferocious. His voice rose. He started shouting while he was driving. I was worried when he lost his control over the steering as he was referring to some instances where my mom was supposed to have hurt his mother. I tried to recollect the happy moments between my father and his mom. There was not even one that I could recollect. Was my father really upset? I had no answer to this.

As we reached home .. I ran into the bedroom where grandma was lying. I did not wash my legs as I was always supposed to. My father was shouting, 'Oun... Oun...'. I just ran in. My grandmother was just like a skeleton covered in a bed sheet. I went inside and leaned on her. She recognized me. There was a sparkle in her eyes. I licked her face, nose..and chin, as I used to do when I was a very young child. I could sense that she was genuinely very happy to see me. I saw the brightness in her eyes. She wanted to speak and tell me something but she could not. Tears started rolling from her eyes. She wanted to hold my hands but failed. I held her hands. When tears began to roll from my eyes and I began sobbing, she just touched my both cheeks with her hands with great struggle and indicated "NO" by nodding her head sideways. I wiped my tears and smiled at her. She also smiled. What a wonderful smile it was. Thereafter a big noise escaped from her mouth..and ...and....she was declared dead by the nurse standing next to her. Someone called my father who rushed there. He started crying ..he was rolling on the ground, not a new sight to me. For every fall of the hat he would do it. He had done it when my mother had taken away the gold jewellery given by his mother to my mom. He had done this, when he suggested that I be admitted to a specific school, whereas my mom had some other school in her mind.. I did not find any difference now. But I did not cry. My grandma's smile came in the way and prevented me from crying. Probably from that day I don't think tears have ever rolled down from eyes.

My father held my hand tightly, and took me to each and every one there and introduced me to each of them. Some elderly lady said, ' Badi -ma (as my grandmother was fondly called) was waiting for her grandson to show her way to heaven.' Suddenly my father took me to his room, and said, "You fool, don't you know the seriousness of situation? Your grandmother is dead and you are not crying.. cry I say.. else, what will people think? I know it is all because of your mother. She might have instructed you not to cry. She has brought you up without any emotions. You are just a paper.. a waste paper. Sometimes I wonder whether you are my son or of that ...xxxx who is your mother's life." His emotions went out of control taking my mom's friend's name.. Suddenly he got very furious and he slapped me and shouted at me, "Get back to your dirty mom.. there is a car and driver waiting for you." He thought I would cry and create a big scene. I did not say anything. I just looked at him for less than a minute and went out. My grandmother's nurse came running, "Such a good boy.. I don't understand how you can beat him. He was so dear to your mother. As long as she could speak, your mother was always talking only about your son. Never did she speak about you or anyone else.. and ..today you are hitting him..who was so dear to your mother.. Chhhheee..!!! God will not forgive you.' She took me in, took out some cream and applied it on my cheek softly. I went and sat inside the car. The driver came and drove me back home. That nurse was more sensible than anyone else. Thank God, a child's world is not merely with its parents alone. There will also be a few strangers in its life who may stand next to the child, to help the child come out of the stifling loneliness. My grandma's nurse was one such.

Looking back at life I sometimes wonder why my father took me to my grandma. Was it for him just a ritual to be followed? I had never seen my father being supportive or loving towards his mother. But I am happy that he took me there. Some memories stay strong and long. That last smile of my grandma has stayed with me forever. It is still with me. Her strong command of "NO" to my tears, has always given me courage. I am thankful to my father for this. Children need a family. We learn many things ..many dos and don'ts from our parents, from our extended family members.. Some people bond with you despite the fact that you are not living with them. Some do not... even if you stay for ever with them under the same roof! Why one is drawn so strongly towards one and why does one try to keep away from another? I can hardly count the number of days I stayed with my grandmother.. or sentences I have spoken to her. But what drew me close to her and her to me was something mysterious. Dynamics of relationship is amazing. What is that strong thread? Blood..? Love..? Kindness? Sense of belongingness? Gratitude? Possessiveness..a subjective feeling that the other person loves you –cares for you..? . I am yet to find the answer.

15

Chapter - 15

I was feeling very despondent missing Badri. The other classmates began to gossip rubbish about him. Someone said, "The Principal kicked him out." Another remarked, 'He is taken away by the police and he is behind bars.' Someone else commented, 'His mama, that is, his mother's brother, (maternal uncle) took him with him to a village to train him in agriculture'. No one dared ask me. Everyone knew that I had a special bonding with him. One day all of a sudden some policemen came to our school. The Principal called me to his chamber and said, 'Badri's father has given a missing complaint and the police will ask you some questions and you should answer politely and they won't harm you.' There were four of them. They started interrogating me. After several questions they came to the point. 'Do you know where Badri has gone?' 'I don't know.' 'Was he upset about anything?' 'I don't know.' 'Where might he have gone? 'I have no idea.' 'What do you know about Badri?' 'He is a good boy..'. 'Why do you say he is a good boy?' 'I did not see anything bad in him.' 'What according to you is "bad"?' 'What is not "good".' The inspector turned to the Principal and said,"It is difficult to talk to this boy..is he arrogant..?

The Principal said, 'No. Not at all ..But ..he...he speaks very little.' The chief of the police said, "hataao iskaaa naam" (remove his name). They asked me to go back to the class room.

Later in the evening the Principal again sent for me and I went to his chamber. He offered me a chair close to him. Closing the door, he said, " Are you missing Badri?" "Yes," I said. 'You also want to go away from this School?' I did not say anything ..but... looked straight into his eyes. I felt as though the Principal understood me. The Principal opened his draw.. took out a neatly maintained file and gave it to me. 'Fill in this application and bring it back to me.' I went through it and asked him, "May I fill it here itself?" The Principal understood the reason behind. Said, 'yes' and walked out. I sat down and filled it with great patience. The Principal returned and looked at it and attached to it his hand written recommendation. He gave his recommendation to me. There was no exaggeration. There was nothing false in it. I had been introduced in the letter. The true "me" had been introduced. I felt very moved. The recommendation letter said what I am. It implied what I am not and can never be. I was surprised as to how some people who have never been communicating with one directly on a day to day basis can understand one so precisely. How do they understand what exactly one wants? How do they listen to what is not being spoken?

Two months' later I was informed by the Principal that I had been selected on a complete student fellowship in a European country. My parents were asked to come. They were literally shocked and surprised. They were both happy too but could not express anything. It was an issue of prestige for them. There was a big function suddenly organized by the Principal the following evening. The committee members were invited. The Deputy Commissioner of the District arrived. I was made to sit next to him on the stage. They all spoke. Someone praised my parents for bringing me up in the right way. They both looked at each other. At the end the Principal stood up. He mentioned the parameters for selection about which I had no idea whatsoever, even while applying. I was astonished that the selection committee chose me. But one sentence the Principal uttered on that day has been etched in my memory through out. "Very few people will have the capacity to move on with life without cribbing. That is his greatest qualification. Reon is one such rare child."

The day on which I had to leave for U.K., my parents came to the air-port. I was surprised to see our Principal. He just patted on my back and said, "Life is beautiful- the world is large. Keep moving. Don't ever forget it, Reon." I just looked deep into his eyes. I felt he was genuinely missing me. I could sense his feelings. I could recognize that he had that feeling which I had when Badri bade goodbye to me. YESSSSSS. I kept moving..

I was told by my parents, separately by each of them, that they had withdrawn the court cases. They had got divorced.

The frequency of their phone calls went on reducing. It was just an obligation which each wanted to discharge diligently. Mom was repeatedly asking me, 'Why don't you speak when I call? Why do you answer in words and not in sentences? I only said, "I am like that mom.. I don't like to talk too much." My father's calls were no different. 'Has anyone asked you not to speak to me..Tell me who that is .. I will show them who I am.. Are you dumb..? Has not God given you a tongue? Why are you making your father suffer? ..Following this was, how he had grown up... what all hardships of life he had to go through ..how my mom spoiled his life ..... on and on..... I felt parents have the capacity to render their children deaf. Are we punching bags for our parents? What are we for our parents?

I received a mail from my Father one day.. 'I am moving on in my life. I am marrying Seema Aunty. Hope you're ok with it.' I sent a brief reply. "Noted. No issues."

Two months after that I received a mail from my mom. 'When your father has moved on in his life, why should I be a dumb ass. I am getting married to Dileep Uncle on Monday. Hope you will not get angry with me.' I replied, "Not at all."

My parents used to get my progress cards regularly. At the end of every year, I used to get a scanned copy of the interview given by my parents to the Press. I was surprised to read many things my parents said as to how they struggled to bring me up. I gradually stopped reading what they said. I knew for sure that I had no control over them. One thing was true. They had really struggled hard. When parents turn away from each other and have nothing but hatred between them and have only been waiting for the children to grow into adults, their life can definitely be nothing short of a struggle. A strange thought occurred in my mind. What would they have said if I had run away from them and school as Badri had done? Why do parents want to take pride in their children's so called accomplishments? Why do they blame each other or everyone else, when the state of affairs is different? Are children in this world only to live up to satisfy their parents? Are they not entitled to possess their own dreams? Why do parents want the children to live their lives? Why do parents live the lives of their children? Don't they have their own? Why do parents want to be the script writers for their children? As these questions began to brew within me, I decided to work on child related laws. 'From Science to Law? Are you sure?' My professor asked me. There was a firm YES from my end. The Honorary Chancellor of our University asked me to meet him. An elderly man of 75 years. I was told by many that he was a highly respected man and his word would be the last one- be it in the university or in the community. The Chancellor was addressed by all in the community as 'CM', short for Complete Man. Everyday hundreds of letters were addressed to him by many. Many had a strange faith that their problems would get addressed by writing letters to the CM about them, as miracles happened when someone approached the CM. As I went to meet the CM, I saw him waiting to receive me at the gate. He greeted me wholeheartedly and led me to his room. "Are you sure of your choice?" He asked me slowly. I said, "YES." "Please go ahead. All the Best." When I stood up and was about to turn towards the door assuming the meeting had concluded, he put his hands on my shoulder and asked, "Is it because you did not have a happy childhood?" I did not answer him but asked him suddenly, "Sir, are you living a happy old age?" To this question of mine he did not answer. I continued in my assertive voice, "I want to know who lives a child's life? Is it the child? Or its parents? Or caretakers? Courts? Judges? Authorities? Any other major?" I want to know how a child grows into an adult. I want to know whether childhood means 'living under the control of a major or majors or much more beyond that? I was surprised. I did not know how I could speak so much. Never ever had I spoken so much with anyone except Badri. Why did I ask so many questions? I was shivering. Suddenly I felt both the hands of the CM laid on my head. I heard him saying, 'Blessed will be your children. Go ahead Reon. I am sure you are on the right path.' At his single command the University did everything to change the line of my studies. I studied Psychology.. I studied Law, Philosophy and Sociology. My publications were appreciated. I became Dr. Reon for others. Once again there was a celebration. Garlands ..photos...news reports.. television interviews started pouring in. I received several hundreds of letters of appreciation from everyone. But ... I noticed that the CM did not congratulate me at all. I had always considered myself to be a person who had overcome expectations. I had identified myself as a person who does not expect anything from others. However, the silence of CM was something that churned me from within. This had never happened to me ever before with anyone or anything. Unable to bear this anxiety, I myself volunteered to take up an appointment with the CM. As I stepped in, the CM stood up from his chair, greeted, and before I could say something he opened his cupboard, removed a sealed bundle and handed it over to me. 'Reon, please go through these letters and get back to me when you find the answers.' Many things which I wanted to ask him remained with me. I nodded my head and came back with the letters. There were several hundreds of them addressed to the CM. Some were written by children, some by parents and friends, hostel wardens, social workers, psychologists, heads of remand homes for children, activists, lawyers, judges, politicians and various organizations. I sorted out all those. The letters written by children and parents shook my conscience. The questions asked by them disturbed me deeply. The narratives they gave led to a world of problems. My Ph.D. did not have an answer to any one of these. I began to question myself, was it the reason why the CM did not congratulate me ? Where do I get solutions to these questions? How do I find solutions? Of what use was my Ph.D.? Why am I Dr. Reon? I went back to the CM and told him that I wanted to start working from the scratch. He just smiled and patted my back with a sign of approval.

16

Chapter - 16

"The letters"

1.My mother had hit my father's mother twice. My mother threatened me to be prepared to meet the same fate if I ever spoke with my father's mother. My father was a mute spectator. The only memories of my mother that I carry with me at the age of fifty are her commandments, "do this, don't do this." Even after I became an adult she was controlling me till my marriage. I decided not to have children. I live justifying my decision. But sometimes, I regret.. . Have I committed a mistake?

2. My father used to do weird things to my mom. Both were naked. My mother was howling and shouting in pain. She was begging my father to at least send me out of the room. He did not agree. He insisted that I should watch how he troubled my mother. I have watched it happen for several years.. . Now I am married. Married for 6 years. My husband is a nice man. But the moment he comes near me to touch me..I scream..I shout.. Why do I see my father in him? Why? Why does it happen to me?

As I completed reading some letters on similar lines, some questions popped up within me. I started making my own notes.

"Some uncherished memories of childhood make other probable sweet moments of life unacceptable."

Do children have control over their parents' behaviour?

How do children know that they should move away from their parents? Where should they go? Who would accept them?

4. My father was a sweet person. He loved me a lot but hated my mother. They always fought with each other. I was asked to stay with my mother by the court. My father was permitted to take me on weekends for three hours. One day I wanted to go for a big job. I remember I was just three years old. My father sat in front of me, cleaned me, and as he was wiping my buttocks, he kissed my 'susu' and also my cheeks, and helped me to put on my inner wears. Then he went inside the bath room, asked me to follow him, as he did not want to leave me alone. He removed his 'susu' out and passed urine. He was looking and smiling at me. Then he came in. We ate food and went to the garden and played. I told everything to my mom. She got wild. She made me tell everyone that my father put his 'susu' on my 'susu'. It had not happened. But I told what I was asked to by my mother. I wanted to sail with my mother. I was under her control rather than under her care. I sincerely felt I was obligated to her. I did not want to disappoint her. I felt, I don't know why, less obligated to my father. No one understood my vulnerable

position. From 3 ½ years to 14 years I repeated whatever I was asked to tell. My father's true statement that he kissed my susu out of sheer love for his daughter and he took me inside the bathroom only to see that I was not left alone in the room where there were an electric stove, a gas stove etc was not appreciated by anyone. My father was not allowed to have any association with me. Today, I saw my mother giving a wash to my son. After wiping him, she held him high above her, and shook him with all her love and kissed his 'susu'. She kissed his cheeks and lips too and dressed him up. If my mom was not wrong how could my father be? I am deeply troubled by my guilt. How do I overcome it? I am unable to sleep, eat or do anything. I am told that my father is dead.. Dear CM, please take me out of this hell.... I told a lie for fourteen years against my father .. to every one—even to court... to please my mother ... Take me out of this guilt.. It is suffocating me. CM, please help. I beg you..

Note: "Why does not a parent know that he/she is causing permanent suffering to the children when they are asked to tell lies about the other parent? Vengeance at what cost?" I started asking myself.

I had always felt that children's voice must be heard because I was deprived of that opportunity. But I had never thought that there is a need to put the system in place to see "how to listen to and understand the true voice of the child." Many a time what was heard was not the voice of the child but that of either of the parents or some others in the tone of the child which is misconstrued as the voice of the child. I started digging deeper. I started working more on empathy. I wanted to comprehend the unsaid rather than the said.

5. I was asked to supervise the visitation given to the father, so that father could have uninterrupted interaction and spend quality time with his son. The child was around 9 years of age. He was freely moving everywhere in the centre., talking desultorily with many. He spoke with me continuously on many issues. Beginning with ice cream , cricket it extended to not going to the temple, striking his friend and then taking him to hospital etc. When his father came, the child came running and sat on my lap hugging me fast. He did not want to see his father. How much-so-ever I tried , the child refused even to look at his father . Try his best as the father did, nothing worked. Mother came in and said, 'When my son was two year old he had seen his father pushing me down, and sitting on my tummy and tightly holding my neck. Which child will come forward to speak to such a father? Haan naa beta? (Isn't it son?)' She sought her son's approval and the son nodded in approval... For years if the child is repeatedly told something by one of the parents against the other parent, and the child has completely believed it (may be it is true or not true) without any second thought, how do I, as a counsellor or facilitator or head of the centre, bring in a shift? How can reproachment be brought in? Why does a child hate one of the parents? Is it just because the parent with whom the child is staying does not like or hates the other parent? Or is it because one strong instance has got stuck deeply in the child's mind? Or is it because the child does not want to take any decision but would like to continue with the status quo? CM please help me.. to help the child .. to help the father.. to assist the court.

Note: I was shocked to know the effect of words on children. The effect of repeated assertions by one parent against the other, the effect of overall control by a parent with whom the child is living, the haunting effect of one single situation on a child.. Who would know the struggle the child is going through to please its parent with whom the child lives, by suppressing a thought which may be genuinely prompting him/her from within asking him/ her not to do so. Who would help the child to reconcile with situations that have happened in the past and move on in life?

6. My father had suspected that my mother was in relationship with another man. He could not digest it. One day he took me out in the pretext of shopping, and brought me to his home country. He had planned everything. He pampered me taking me to different places. There was entertainment everywhere. My mother struggled hard to get me back but failed. I said whatever I was asked to by my father. I declared that I would like to be with my father but never with my mother. I do not know why I said so. But am sure I did not want to displease my father who gave all enjoyments in a short period of few months. I felt obligated. I could not think too far .. far beyond my comfort levels. The court verdict was in favour of my father. I can still remember the broken heart -feelings of my mother on that day of judgment. Later my father shifted himself and me to his home country. He put me under the care of his old ailing parents and his brothers and their wives, who had no love for me. My mother could not afford to come from one country to another to meet me often. Once, when

she came, she was not given access to me. When it was given, I was ordered by my father not to speak to her. My mother felt that I had forgotten her.. CM, I have not ..I have not.. . I was asked to tell everyone, “She is dead for me.” How can that be? But I did it.. I did it.. I don’t know why I did it. I don’t know why I did not oppose it. I grew up and became independent. I saw my father having affairs with different women. I understood what was it all that happened around me. How could I reverse the clock? I went to my mother. My mother was suffering from early dementia. She could not recognise me. She died.... not so much because of her illness as because I had killed her ...I had killed her... Because I had told everyone that she was not there in my world.” CM, I feel utterly humiliated and ashamed .. I want to kill myself. I see how my wife cares for the children, how she struggles and how she disciplines our children.. I see how a mother does what she does. What should I do now? Isn’t there a mechanism to make the persons in authority understand what exactly is meant by the phrase “best interest“ and “paramount interest”? Can they be made to understand that they need to learn a lot to know what exactly a child needs? I strongly feel that they work at the superficial level of understanding children’s wants but not their needs which cannot be expressed in words but can only be understood, which cannot be negotiated but can only be satisfied.

Note: This was too much for me. I thought that a child should always be heard. But here I was exposed to a different situation altogether. Here was a situation where the child said, ‘It would say something. But don’t go by the words expressed by it.’ I thought understanding the needs of a child is the thing we should focus on.

There were many such letters. Each spoke volumes. Some letters were by devastated children. Some were by grandparents. Some were by parents who confessed as to how they failed in bringing up their children. Some had shared their helpless situations due to which they had given up on the custody battle before the courts.

In some letters there was nothing but blame. Some of the letters were filled with accusations. Whether it was guilt, shame, powerlessness, helplessness, feeling of insecurity, disappointment, anger, anxiety, pain everything revolved around the individual who had written the letter. Many letters revolved around what should not have happened, what ought to have been avoided or prevented. Some letters spoke in volumes about the continued agony of childhood constantly troubling an individual even after growing old. Some wanted to pour out. Some expected remedies. Some wanted to take revenge. Some expressed their disappointments and helpless situations.

17

Chapter - 17

Letter from Jania was different. It read..

Dear CM,

Thank you for taking time to read my letter.

I am one of the rarest of children. I don't remember having walked after my third year. Before that I remember having toddled a few steps . I would hardly take 4-5 steps and I would sink down. My parents started growing anxious. My brother had started walking at the age of two. My parents waited with patience. Visits to different specialised doctors, astrologers of high reputation, temples across the country ..... were all part of my day to day life. I remember how my mother and father and at times my brother would carry me to all these places. Nothing worked out. I was immobile for all practical purposes. My parents and brother showered all their love, affection and energy to see to it that I got the best that I could enjoy and experience in life with all the limitations associated with my body. I am completely wheel chair bound as I am writing this letter at the age of thirty. Ever since my tenth year I have been constantly on the wheelchair. I have overheard doctors telling my aunt about my mother, "Your sister in law is amazing .. But for her this child would have been a vegetable by now." So much of love, affection, commitment not just from my parents and brother but from the members of the extended family of both my parents made me accept life as a challenge. I was a voracious reader. I cultivated the habit of writing too. My friends at school and college were extremely helpful. I remember the first day when my mother strove to carry me half way to the first floor of my college, whereas I had to reach to the third floor. Two boys came from nowhere. Put me on a chair and carried me to the third floor. This happened every day for five years. I don't know how much grateful I should be to this world for all these. I remember my father fighting with someone when they had not permitted me to write the exam in the ground floor. Spinal Muscular Atrophy was the peculiar disease I was diagnosed with. On the academic side I was an achiever. Step by step I went ahead. I am continuing my research on topics related to persons struggling hard to cope with disability. As I am writing this, I know that I will not survive for long. My lungs have been failing. My neck is not stable and I find it difficult to position myself. I feel very disturbed when my parents, my brother and loving sister in law join their hands struggling hard to take me to bed, to the rest room and bathroom, to my college, work place and conference halls. I can understand their pain. I have seen them sacrificing their own right to enjoyment. I can sense the feeling of guilt in my parents. I have overheard them saying, 'What sin have we committed to cause so much of pain to this child?' They have never even asked once,

"What sin have we committed to suffer so much because of this child?' Their only concern has been that I should not suffer. I can strongly feel that any child's suffering would be the suffering of the parents too.

I have been helped by my brother even in changing my carefree pads during my monthly periods. I have seen him controlling his tears in front of me, and getting into the bath room and crying there pouring his heart out.

Dear C.M, people call us special children. Or... persons with special needs. As far as I am concerned I would say that I was really a very SPECIAL CHILD for my parents, a special sister for my brother and a special person for all others with whom I have come in touch. True, at times I had felt that I am missing so much in this world because of my disability. But I have also seen many with good health and wealth and yet cribbing and suffering offering excuses of their own for their self-created and at times self-imagined sufferings. Unfortunately, many forget to count on their blessings. I did not want to be one such. As I grew older I understood that there is a purpose behind every life. If I am born like this, and if I am designed by the higher principle to be like this, it is for a purpose. May be it is to show to the world that such people can also receive, experience and reciprocate unconditional love. Would I have received the taste of unconditional love without reciprocation of any kind from my end, if I had not been a special child? I don't have the exact answer for it. I am blessed. I am truly blessed to have such wonderful family, friends, strangers who have given me everything through their empathy to its core and treasured by me as a precious possession. The world is beautiful. I have learnt to see and enjoy the beauty of this world without trying to watch it through the glasses of disability.

I know for sure that the condition of my health cannot be improved by any stretch of imagination. By the time you read this letter, I may not even be alive. I learnt to accept life as it is. But I looked at the other opportunities available in this world for me to see and enjoy the beauty of life. I have enjoyed it. I grew very strong academically. My achievements have been recognised, and I have become financially independent. Sir, I would say that financial independence gives a kick to persons like us. My mother always said, "You are a fighter—fight –fight till the last breath." I have followed that one mantra. As long as that mantra remains with me I can fight. I can fight against the illusion that "There is no hope for special children." Mr. C.M, everything has to come to an end. Even the said Mantra is trying to move away from me. I know I am reaching my last days. I have a humble request:

Can you please pass on the Mantra given to me by mother to the entire world of "Special Children." This one Mantra is specially designed for people like me.

I am enclosing a cheque for the entire balance in my account for this cause. How you carry it forward is left to you. CM, I have faith in you.. I trust YOU.

18

Chapter - 18

Reflection:

Jania's letter was a revelation to me. I understood the power of letter writing. Can a single letter change one's entire perspective of life? The answer is a clear "YES".

The thoughts were scattered. But every line of the letter when independently read communicated what was not expressed in words. Jania's letter opened a different window to peep into the world.

Jania's letter assured me of the power of the glimpses of hope. There was light in her life. There was no 'inexhaustible gloom' as others would have assumed her to be living in. Jania's heart filled with pure love pure love could see it. Pure unconditional love of the entire family, friends and the entire world was bright enough to make her life completely enjoyable and meaningful. Jania demonstrated to the world that there is special space in this special world for special children. Jania had replaced all odds with Hope. She gradually added her determination to live and explore the beauty of the world.

She committed herself to working for a larger cause moving beyond her so called limitations. She gave a clear message that the beauty of the world is not only for a chosen fortunate few. It is for all. Once you are born in this world.. you have the right to live till your death. That right gives you the right to enjoy your life as a human being. Jania's parents believed in giving that space to Jania. They understood well that the world has sufficient room for such children too. They understood very well that the world is not a small space. The accommodative potential of the world was clearly understood by them.

I understood my mission. I learnt from Jania that there are ways children can be happy. There are ways children can cherish from their childhood. There is no emptiness in any child's life. The world around should be shown to children. Children should be brought in touch with the true "FAMILY" . The entire world is a "FAMILY for children.

After reading several such letters I knew why the CM did not congratulate me when I was conferred with the doctorate.

I knew where I had failed. I began to comprehend that 'Your achievements are of no value if they do not add value either to your life or to others' lives.'

ÞÞÞ

19

Chapter - 19

Human nature has no defined boundaries. When we cannot tell why a father or mother does what he/she does how can we try to control a child's behaviour? I remember someone having said it rightly, 'There cannot be any law for morality.' Why does the chemistry between two persons get disrupted is a question with no definite answer. It is a surprising truth that each individual's life is different. Each human being is different. Each child is different. Even though born to same parents, one child differs from another. What does a child actually need? This cannot be compromised with what either of the parents wants. Cannot a child be allowed to live its life on its own without being controlled by both or either of the parents? How can a child enjoy his/her childhood if he is controlled in the pretext of disciplining it? Several such questions started haunting me. I began to review my life in retrospect for the first time.

My dad and mom were two different individuals. They had their own strong likes and dislikes which they mistook as rights and wrongs. Each tried to thrust his/ her individual choices on the other. It did not work both being strong personalities. But I was there in between. Each one wanted to have complete ownership over me, only to exercise ownership over the other through me. Unfortunately, both failed. I stood in their lives being a mute spectator. I watched them both struggling from morning till evening, only to come back home to reflect as to what should be done to win over the other. Marriage for them was a platform of competition. I did not sail with either of them but I always sailed with the situation. I accepted life as it came. What other choice would children like me have? I had a unique trait of enjoying observation. I spent more time looking around. I have never been interested in knowing why people did what they did, or why they spoke what they spoke. But I was truly interested in observing what they were doing and/ or not doing. At times I took notice of what others said or did not say. If my mom asked me to go with her, I went. When my dad asked, I followed him. If both of them had a fight, I waited for them to agree or disagree as to what I should be doing. By my very nature, I wanted to avoid confrontations. I felt surrendering to the situation was a safe space for me. I was like a teddy bear. I could be folded and plied in any way. I did not want to justify myself with others. I always lived in my own world to which no one had an easy access. I tried to protect that personal space of mine. I was safe within myself but not with either or both my parents. Minni, butterflies and Badri were the only exceptions. Probably that is the reason why I could not and cannot be judgmental on my parents. So many have asked me, 'Do you hate your mom or father? Whom do you hate more? Why do you hate?' I hated none. They have also asked me, 'Do you love your mom more than your father or your father more than mom? ' I wanted to say, 'I did not love either of them.' To be honest, I did not understand what love is throughout my childhood. Do you love someone? If you miss someone when the person is absent, then there is love! I love Minni, Butterflies and Badri. If you are saddened if someone moves away from you, then there is love. I love my father's mom, Badri, Minni, Butterflies. If some come to your mind often, who for sure are not the ones whom you hate, then those are loved by you. Then yes .. I love Minni, Badri and Butterflies. Minni, Badri and Butterflies have always been loved by me.

Questions began to crop up in me one after the other. It is unfortunate that children who are already in a more disadvantageous position than the ones questioning them, are often shot questions like whether they love their father or mother or both or whom they hate and why? Who has to define what is it meant by 'love' or 'hate' for a child? Does the one who questions the child define what 'love' or 'hate' would mean? It is surprising to see someone say, 'We should see to it that a child is loved by both the parents and the child loves both of them'. Is it practically possible? How would you do it? How would you measure love or hatred?

20

Chapter - 20

All of us went to Olympic National Park. Bram, the first one, was very excited as he had a chapter on this National park in his syllabus. When Minni and I were having a private conversation to take a vacation so that we could get settled without carrying the luggage of the past, Bram peeped in and said, “Can we go to Olympic National Park? It is not too far from Seattle, I have done all the research.” He quickly went in and handed over the map too. Minni looked at him in disapproval. He was regarding me expectantly. I could not deny him. I was just speaking to myself, ‘Our idea was going out to enjoy the vacation. If someone else’s purpose could be achieved by this why say ‘No’. I told Minni, ‘Even I have not visited it. Let us go if you have no objection.’ We all went on a road trip from Seattle. Minni said, Badri always used to say, ‘The older one is a clone of Reon.’ I smiled. I could understand why Badri had named the first son as Bram. B for Badri, R for Reon, A for “another” and M for Minni. Badri knew very well as to how I had been named. He had always praised our Principal on that. But I was a little bit puzzled and equally disturbed about the “A” in BRAM. I guessed that “A” would stand for “ANOTHER”. Knowing Badri, I could confirm that Badri never wanted to evade anyone's role in life. I heard Minni repeatedly quoting Badri saying, "Avoiding is not good. It haunts. One whom you have presumed to have avoided, will constantly be with you. You can't avoid some at least from your thoughts. They will perpetually be with you." Badri did not do away with anyone. But, I always tried either to eliminate people from my list, or tried to avoid them and failed constantly.' Minni said, 'Do you know Ray.. there was not even a single conversation between us in which you were not present.' I could resonate with Minni well on this point. It is true at times persons who are not physically with us will be emotionally with us all through. I have experienced it. Minni and Badri were always with me. Now this "A" is also there. He is there because he is in Bram and the other two children. "A" enters and exits now and then. But "A" cannot be eliminated. Strangely enough, there was an "A" in all the three names of the little ones. I did not want to know who that "A" is or was. I did not want to probe deep into it.

Bram was taking a picture of the trees. The little ones were interested in taking their own pictures. Hoh Rain Forest had many huge trees. Hall of Mosses was an amazing sight. The major portion of the huge trees was seen covered with very huge lumps of moss. Unable to withhold the curiosity, Rebam, the second one, asked the elder one at once, "Bram, the moss has already covered the trees so much.. over a period of time that will pervade all the original trees. Camouflaged by the moss, the trees will not be seen at all. No one will know how the trees were originally. Is it not unjust? Bram ignored that question as he was too busy taking photos and making notes. I looked at Minni and found her face turning completely black. I did not ask her anything. I had learnt that when people seem to be disturbed it is better to allow them some time to settle. Minni did not speak even a single word with me during the next few hours. She was giving mono-syllabic answers to the children. It was as though she was not with us at all.

We moved to Ruby Beach. The children were playing. Minni asked the youngest one not to go near the water but play in sand. I sat watching the children. Minni came and sat next to me. She did not look at my face. It was as though she was trying to trace the horizon. Slowly, she said, " Ray..., I want to speak to you....."

She always addressed me as Ray... May be for her I was a Ray..

She spoke in a low voice.

"Ray...,it's nice of you that you have decided and made all arrangements to move away from that city to another along with me and the three little ones. Ray, I am hesitant. I am deeply worried. Are we not trying to cloud you? Please think over ...You will be lost.. lost completely. Badri would never expect me to do it. I cannot be dishonest to you or to Badri either. Ray, please leave us. Leave us and take your life forward."

I was shocked. I never expected Minni to say this to me. How could she not trust me..? How could she have even entertained this doubt? I was trying to find out how and where I failed in convincing that my family always had 'Me, Badri and Minni'. And that any one associated with Badri and Minni would be part of my family. When trust gets shattered everything else does. It struck to me for the first time that 'If I feel that I am trustworthy, it would be of no use. The others should feel that I am trustworthy for them.' I noticed that there is something shallow within me . That...started making me turn topsy turvy.

Regaining control over myself I asked her, 'Minni, why are you disturbed so much? '

Minni said in the lowest of her voices, 'Did you hear Rebam's question..? I am afraid one fine day.. moving around all the four of us, you will be completely lost. You will not have any identity of your own. You will be only my husband, God Father for my children ..even though ..actually....actually you are not. I am still more worried because what you have achieved in all these years may get lost in the process. I do not want that to happen. A person like you, Mr. Reon, coming forward to stretch beyond the limits is making me feel too small... Too small.. I am feeling guilty. I feel guilty because I am making you move from the pinnacle to nowhere. Never did I feel so guilty. Never ever. Even when I lay naked in bed with many men...." Minni started sobbing. I could feel her spleen churn with every word she spoke.

I could understand the origin of her doubt. "Hall of Mosses". How powerful is nature! In a minute it can make any one feel smaller and smaller. However, I knew for sure that the same nature can be reassuring too. When one feels completely lost, it is the all-pervading nature that can give a safe, cosy and comforting hug.

I drew Minni closer to me. She laid her head on my shoulders and I slowly whispered to her.. "Minni, your understanding of moss is wrong. Moss grows on another plant without harming it. It is said somewhere that moss is effective at absorbing sounds. May be, the tree is valued. May be, the tree feels valued because it has allowed the moss to grow on it. I do not know much about the science related to plants. May be, I am wrong.. But I would go with that understanding. I have always understood nature to be reassuring. I would continue to understand it that way. I beg you Minni, you and Badri have always been value additions to me. The children are now included in that picture. I want to see how the children become true adults naturally, on their own, without losing anything from their childhood. I want to be a part of our children's lives. I want the children to be a part of my life. I feel, only then I can be a complete human being. There is a void in me. There is something which is very large, missing in me. I want to get it. I want to experience it. All that I can request you now is, 'Allow me to grow..allow me to evolve.'

Minni noticed tears rolling down my cheeks. She hugged me. She slowly licked the tears. I can count and tell when I cried. I did not often. But when Minni started licking the tears I felt the same feeling which I had years ago on a day when Minni and I were very young and a butterfly had come and sat on my cheek. I felt so excited. There was completion. I had thought that 'that butterfly' had died and it would never come. I was wrong. I and only I could see that and I could feel that butterfly coming back.. I and only I knew for sure that it was the very same butterfly. I don't think butterflies die .. At least some do not.... I said to myself.

My thoughts could have stretched further. Minni said, 'Ray.. I want to give you the whole of myself. Before you accept me, ..I want to show you every part of mine. Are you ready? Please allow me,' she pleaded. I could not say 'NO'.

♡♡♡

21

Chapter - 21

Minni's narrative unwound thus. I felt she virtually went into a trans-mode as she went on explaining..

Ray .., do you remember the contractor under whom my mother worked for many years? That dark, well-built man? May be, he was in his fifty plus when both of us had seen him. I am sorry to say this.. but...when your mother came and complained to him that you were being spoiled by my company and the only way to avoid that was to see to it that my mother was removed. That is how we were evicted. That gentleman contractor asked us to move out overnight. I was not allowed to take my things. Many of our clothes, small vessels, given to us over many years by many were asked to be left there itself. When I cried my mother said, 'I cannot carry more than a bag or two and your brothers. Leave everything here.' When I went in to pick up my doll, the contractor kicked me on my butts. The contractor gave some money to my mother and ordered her to shift to a different place. He called someone and asked them to set our hut on fire. Everything turned into ash within no time...right in front of our eyes. Heaps of mud came from somewhere. The entire site was cleared. It was as though nothing with which we had lived for years and years was ever there. Looking at me, he said, "All the worthless things stored unnecessarily had made the locality unclean." I felt very bad and helpless. How could someone else not in our place decide what is not important and precious for us? Ray.. I always hated someone taking charge of someone else's life. Don't we have the right to live our life the way we want to..? The contractor did not understand what the loss of things so very precious for the child would mean to the child. My mother knew but she was helpless. I could feel the pain in her eyes. Her helplessness was obvious when she asked me to leave everything there. I did not want my mother to feel hurt. I pretended as though I did not value my belongings much. Ray, as a child I still remember how I pretended to hide my true emotions. When you notice that the pain of someone whom you love is so much greater than your pain, you sacrifice your pain. It is unfortunate that a child is made to sacrifice experiencing its own pain as it is going through the experience the pain of someone else.

Ray, I remember travelling almost three nights and a day. Mother said, 'We are relocating.' I asked her whether we could stay in the same town in a different place. I remember mother telling me, "Minni, you do not understand the language that money speaks. Let us take life as it comes. People like us will have no option than to surrender. We need to surrender to everyone and everything. It does not matter. I am hopeful that your lives will be brighter one day.' She kissed my brother madly. Rich people live on money. The poor survive on hopes. My mother was not an exception. I remember sleeping near the railway station on the roadside for more than three days. That is when my mother met Rajan, a mason. He assured my mother the same old job that she was doing. A different hut. The same routine.. Me and brothers being there from morning till evening and mother coming home tired in the evening. We all were waiting to see what my mother would bring home for us to eat. After her work with the mason, she would work as a maid in the house of the mason and his neighbour. She would bring home the leftovers given by them. After all of us ate she would eat if anything was left. We never bothered to ask her..neither me ..nor my brothers..whether she had eaten something in the afternoon or not. I was taught, to raise my brothers meticulously...to do household chores..to cook, to clean. My mother put my brothers to school under some scheme. We were not asked to pay the school fees. They gave them afternoon meals also. This relieved both my mother and me a lot. I was much older than my brothers. I did not have the guts to ask my mother to show me how the school looked. Ray.. when you know you cannot afford something, you will not even want to see them ..don't you? I knew there would be no point in asking my mother to get me admitted to school. I was sure that it was impossible any way. That was it with me. School was something which I could not even dream. Even to this day I am surprised and unable to understand why even dreams of children also get controlled by situations. Some children are afraid of dreaming. Ray I was one. My brothers never wanted me or my mother to go near their school for whatsoever reasons of their own. They had their own justifications.

Ray..day by day I watched my mother growing very weak. Little by little she was sinking. She slowly pushed me into maid's job as I did not fit into doing anything that was part of the construction work. I had no other option than do it. With my first month's earning I found a tattoo woman and got this Butterfly tattoo etched on my shoulders. I was very happy. It cost me too much. But I always wanted to have YOU on my shoulders. I saw my mother too weak to go out to work. I begged the mason to take her to a doctor. He refused. He said it would cost him too much. I asked my mother, "How do we get more money?" Ray.. I remember her telling me.... 'Let us think about money when you want something at any cost and you cannot live without getting it, or when you want money not to lose something which is very important to you.' I knew what I wanted. "I wanted my mother's health. I did not want to lose her at any cost. I wanted to save her at the cost of everything else in my life. "For the first time, I went all alone to the mason's office. He promised to give me money if I slept with him. He said I would not get pregnant as he had undergone surgery for sterilization and my mom would not know about it. He said he would give me money as long as my mom was alive. He would assure the best medication to my mother. I felt the proposal was good. Either way I was sure that even if I had taken ten odd jobs I would not be able to provide for mom's illness. The mason also assured that he would not make me feel the pain. I went back home and asked mom whether she wanted to live and why he wanted to live. She said, "If I die there will be none to take care of your brothers. I have morbid fear that once I am gone you will be taken away, moved away. I want to live for the sake of your brothers." I was in a way shocked to know, "I was never there. I was not included at all. My mother spoke only of my brothers. Why? Why did she do so? Why was I not at all there in my mother's thoughts?" Ray, even to this day I don't know the answer to this question. I did not ask her the reason. 'What would you do to bear the pain ?' I asked her slowly patting her cheeks. She said in her faint, failing voice, " Surrender. Surrender without questioning. Keep your eyes tightly shut. Assume that you have accepted the situation. That is the only way to get rid of any pain." I decided to surrender. Surrender to Mason Rajan. Because though I was not there in my mother's frame of reference, she was there pervading my life. I was not prepared to lose her at any cost. For me, my mother was everything. I did not bother whether I was important for her or not. For me, she was everything.

I went back to the mason. Surrendered. Surrendered without questioning. Next day when the ambulance came near our home to take mom, I was busy packing . As me and the mason put our mom on the ambulance bed, my mom held my face in her hand, looked deep into my eyes. She found out...Ray... she found out ...she found what I had done... . I know what all she intended to tell me... she did not speak. Not even a single word. Her hands slipped from my cheek all of a sudden. When people do not find words to communicate ..it is very hard to digest. Everything cannot be communicated through words. Her silence spoke volumes. What all a mom would speak to her loving daughter who went behind money to get what she wanted the most ...I could hear. In a way I felt I disappointed my mother. But again I wondered how else I would have saved my mother. What else could I have done? At an age when I was considered still a child I tried to climb the mount Everest. I wanted to achieve... A child's dream to achieve something is different Ray. But a child's goal mission and effort are different. I gave all of myself to stand up out my goal. My mission was to save my mother. The ambulance driver was getting restless. We moved to the hospital. Strangely my mother stopped speaking completely. Even when I asked her to speak she would not. The doctors told me that she had taken a call not to speak, even though she could. I could understand why she had chosen not to speak... She did not know that her silence spoke volumes to me. I wanted my mom to be alive. I did everything to get money to keep her alive. My mom did everything possible from her end to stop me from spending money on her. She did not co-operate with the doctors in any manner. She was on the hospital bed like a piece of plywood. She forgot everything. She even forgot to recognize my brothers who would occasionally come to meet her. After struggling for a year she died. The mason had spent a huge sum of money . He stood by his words. I am thankful to him. Ray, isn't life all about bargaining? We exchange something or the other with different people, at different times for different reasons. We justify what we should get and at what cost.

I made it clear to the mason that our contract should end. He agreed gracefully. I came back home. It was worse than a cemetery. There was ugly silence. There was nothing left for me. I questioned myself if I had come back home. Home is something where you feel like getting back to. I understood it was not my home. I was almost used to sleeping next to my mother in her hospital room except for the two or three hours sleeping next to the mason. There was a total vacuum. Living without any purpose is horrible. It becomes too suffocating. It was at that time my brothers came and told me that they wanted to pursue their education further as the schooling was over, and I had to arrange for money. Now I took up another mission. To fulfil my mother's wish, to see to it that my brothers settled well in life. But one thing is true, the true happiness a child gets in fulfilling the wishes of its mother is unique. I experienced that happiness when I decided to get on to this mission.

I went back to the mason. He said he did not have so much money with him but that he could show me other avenues. I started sleeping left, right and centre with any one brought by the mason. I grew reasonably comfortable with money. I slowly started recognising that the time had come to get what I wanted to have for myself in this world. I wanted to have kids. Ray.. I was told we are bound to be born in this world until we attain complete divinity. Till then we keep taking births in this world. Every soul looks for a place to come to this earth. Why not give the best place for the deserving souls.. May be it would look too childish or meaningless for many. I always thought motherhood is unique. In all the different roles I have seen in this world, mother's role is the best. Everyone should pray the higher principle to give them an opportunity to be a mother, at least once. It helps an individual to evolve completely. I always had a question in my mind. Had my father been a responsible man.., which he was not, according to many.. would our lives have been different? Could my mother have given us better lives if she had not surrendered herself to the situation which she was forced to be in? I always heard my mom thanking my father for having given her the best gifts in the form of me and my brothers. I never heard her complaining against anyone. She never complained against my father also. My mother gave me her pure love. She could do it because she had no complaints against anyone against anything. Love is something which one can experience by loving and not by being loved. I wanted to experience that pure love experienced by mothers. I wanted someone whom I could love, love deeply... very profoundly.. as I loved my mom.. I loved you too Ray. I loved you. I never had any connect with my brothers. I don't know why it was so ..I always felt obligated to them. Honestly speaking I did not love them. Our relationship was too mechanical and more transactional.

I decided to get pregnant. I am mother of three children. If you ask me who their fathers are.. the honest answer would be " I do not know." I did not even want to find out . The "A" in all my three children's names would stand for that 'Another Person', whoever was responsible for their birth biologically. As the children were getting older, I thought I should put a full stop to what I was doing. I knew my beautiful sexy figure would not say "no". Still I thought I should shift the gear before the children came to their senses.

22

Chapter - 22

It was during that time that a strange man came in one day. The mason told me that this rich man was a bit weird. But if 'I click' in the bargain my life would get settled for ever. He came, took me to his posh bungalow. Then he went in to have a shower. I was watching the beautiful garden. He came from behind and hugged me. Tried to kiss me .. and he had not even come close to my lips but suddenly withdrew himself at which I was surprised. Slowly he opened a dialogue with me. As I sat next to him, I started arranging the envelopes and papers scattered on the small expensive table. He found me looking at the windows often. 'Do you love gardens?' he asked and moved towards the windows to remove the curtains. Looking at my broad smile, he climbed on a small stool and opened the windows too. I had always come across people closing the windows as soon as we entered the room. For all men I have come across the woman near mattered much. Rather, there was nothing else that mattered to them.. the body...mattered most. Here was this weird person who opened the windows to see to it that my concerns were addressed. I went near the window. Stood next to him. I held his hands and said,

"Thank you so much.' He said we could walk for a while in the garden if I was OK with it. We both took a long walk. He explained to me why he was interested in trees and plants and flowers. He said he did not listen to people but would always listen to nature. He said, 'Man's best companion is nature. Human beings are no match to it. Nature speaks to you.. it listens to you. But you need to learn the language of nature. It is unique. It takes a life time at times to learn from nature . But it is worth the effort. My ultimate aim in life is to get merged with nature. I love nature. I love it so much that I feel ecstatic as though I am in love with it. I know for sure that nature does not expect me to love it. It does not bother whether I love it or not. It has no complaints against me or anyone else either. No expectations at all. What a wonderful way of reciprocating one's love! May be someone would say it is one way love... But I am sure it is not. I want to attain that climactic moment where I am one with the nature.' I giggled, as he was going on and on. He became self-conscious and suddenly very serious. He continued, 'I know you must be wondering, then, why the hell am I behind people like you?' In fact, that was my question. He said, "I want to ensure that my statement is true. Secondly, and deep within me, I am yet to find that state of climax. If I can find a better companion than nature, I am open for it." I felt some thing unique in this person. Some people carry you to a different altitude altogether, very easily very quietly. I found one such in him . I tried in between to hug him twice and every time I moved my lips near to his, he came forward but suddenly withdrew himself. In the fourth attempt he said, "Something in me is strongly opposing me.. I don't know what it is and why it is resisting. This has never happened to me ever before."

I did not respond. I only remembered what the mason had said, “He is a weird man . If you click with him your life will get settled.” I just brushed aside what all he said but decided that the mason was right in a way and was wrong too. I felt he was indeed a weird man. But I also felt he was a ‘different man.’

As we entered the room we had a luxurious dinner. He offered me drinks. I refused. He was surprised. ‘Can you give your best without a drink?’ I said, ‘Yessss. When you surrender yourself completely to a cause, that gives you the greatest kick . You don’t need anything external to intoxicate you.’ He gave a strange look which conveyed to me what was in his mind. ‘Here is a person more weird than myself.’ We both suddenly burst out laughing. By then he had decided. He wanted to have me. He took one drink after another. Suddenly he pushed me very hard to the bed. Put himself over me. Tried to remove my deep necked shirt. He was not letting me take it out. He wanted to remove it himself .. One of the shoulders came off easily. As he moved to my right shoulder his eyes fell on the butterfly tattoo. All of a sudden he jumped up and sat on the bed. He stared at the butterfly repeatedly. Time and again he returned to look at the butterfly and my face. He moved his hands over the butterfly ..very carefully, very delicately as though he was caressing the edge of a jasmine flower and running through it... By then I had decided that he was really a weird person. Suddenly he asked me, “Are you Minni?” I was shocked.. No one had known me by that name. Not even the mason. I did not answer. He himself said, ‘YESSS. I am sure you are Minni. That is why I was unable to touch you.. I was unable to do that with you.. You are Minni, your butterfly on the shoulder cannot lie. Don't sit dumb to hide everything. Can you at least tell me that you know Reon? 'Ray.., I was shocked to hear your name from this weird person. Something in me stopped me from lying. I nodded. "Yesss. But we lost touch with each other when we were young." Then slowly he introduced himself as BADDYSON. I could understand and got confirmed that Ray.. he was your good friend Badri.

ÞÞÞ

23

Chapter - 23

Life is never plain, it offers surprising twists and shifts. Where, when and how we get to see what types of curves, edges, ups and downs no one can tell us. Everyone meets such shifts. It is unique to each individual. Two people walking together along the same path may experience varied shifts and turns. Some people keep moving in circles even on a plain path. It is not just the path that is accidental. Even our moves too. Choices make a world of difference.

I made the choice of moving and settling down with Badri. I told him my motive. I did not want to hide anything. He gladly agreed. We got married. Both of us were clearly aware that we did not know why we were getting married. But both of us did not find any reason as to why we should not be getting married. Often, 'Why should we not?' rather than 'Why should we?' brings us to good decisions. Getting married to Badri was one such good decision of my life.

Badri gave the children utmost sense of security. He chose their names. He insisted that every name should have me, you and Badri in it. And unexpectedly he included "A". He said he would not want to miss " A" because , I did not have anything against that "A" . One thing I learnt from Badri is being grateful to everyone and everything. He always said, 'Not being grateful is something. It is tolerable. But being ungrateful should never be tolerated.' I felt it all through my journey with him. He lived committed to this throughout. It is difficult to find people living up to what they say. Badri was an exception.

All that neither I nor the children could have ever expected in our lives was assured by Badri. My life truly got settled. I had rightly clicked the right button. We were leading a luxurious and very comfortable life. There was no dearth of anything that was materialistic. All at the cost of Badri. Slowly, I began to feel that Badri was not getting anything in return. I have seen him looking sheepishly at my shoulders. One day, for the first time, I found him shouting at me when I wore a sleeveless blouse. He raised his voice and said, "You better change your foolish dress styles. Never wear a sleeveless blouse, as long as I am alive." Why was he disturbed by the butterflies I did not know. I noticed that whenever he saw the butterflies on my shoulder he would get disturbed, and at times agitated too. I could not negotiate this. I was feeling guilty that I was unable to give Badri anything from our marriage. I decided to get the butterflies removed. The decision was not an easy one. But when you take a hard decision you try to give many justifications in support of your decision. This decision was one such. This was almost like the decision I had taken on a mission to save my mother.

I surrendered myself to my decision. I began to reflect, 'I had no fascination for butterflies. I had a fascination for you, and you had a fascination for butterflies. I had butterflies tattooed on my shoulders as a token of my fascination for you. How strange all this was?' "We do many things and do these at times not because we like or do not like those, but because we have profound liking for someone who likes or who does not like those." Because I had liked you I had butterflies tattooed on my shoulders. Because I liked Badri, I did not like the butterflies to continue to be on my shoulders. My decision got solidified. Reasons help decisions consolidate. I consulted many beauticians. They all said that tattoos put many years ago cannot be removed. I consulted the best of the plastic surgeons. He said something could be worked out through skin grafting. I agreed. Money never bothered me. I had it in abundance. I got admitted myself to a hospital when Badri was out of country for a week. I had left a small personal note about my surgery.

It was all set. I was about to be on the surgery table in the next hour, suddenly the door opened with a bang and Badri dashed in. He held me tightly and looked straight into my eyes. Whispered a stringent warning, 'Never ever try to play with butterflies.' It was a strong warning which could not be ignored by me. I knew what Badri meant when he said it. I had to come back home without undergoing surgery. A week passed by. Neither of us spoke to each other. Slowly he narrated to me what had happened once when Sandeep tried to kill the butterflies with Reon opposing and Badri had intervened. I asked him if he liked butterflies and if so, why? He said that he did not have anything on his own to like or hate butterflies. But he liked butterflies because he likes you and you like butterflies. Ray.. do you know what he said..the only person who always comes before his eyes next only to his mom is Reon that is you. Whenever he sees a butterfly in any form, he feels as though Reon is physically present with him. That is why he said.. he was unable to have physical relationship with me. He said, ' Minni... I beg you never to try to come physically close to me.' He also said that I belong..completely.. to Reon and not to him. And, that...that... he would see to it that I am handed over to you, of course, with my consent.

Ray .. today I do not want you to believe me..or believe whatever I am telling you. I want you to understand something very clearly here. I have nothing to receive from you. Now that my brothers are also on their own and I have the least connect with them, I don't need much money. Whatever Badri has kept is more than enough. Please understand that there is also nothing that I can give you in our relationship. When the little one asked the older one a question about moss pervading the entire tree ..or even the forest, .. I thought if you take us all with you, you would be losing your identity. There may be some give and take between the moss and the trees. But there can be nothing between us. Between me and you. Ray... leave us here. Look forward to your career. You will always be in my heart. Badri came in my life and overtook you. But he never tried to remove you from my heart. In fact he secured a safe place for you in my heart, irrespective of whether you wanted to be there or not. Now Badri may think that he has moved away. No, he is still there. Ray.. I want you to know that, 'There cannot be Minni without Badri'. Badri will always be there with me. He will be there as the father of my children. The children know that I am their mother. Badri will be their father for ever, even if I reveal the fact that I don't know who their respective fathers are, they would say for them Badri is their father. My fear is ..Ray... where will you be in the picture? I do not want you to be insignificant by not being in the picture. Leave us alone....Move away. Please... Please Ray... Please... ' Minni started crying. She was uncontrollable. I did not try to say anything.

24

Chapter - 24

I was not without questions. 'Why?' regarding some aspects of life haunts every individual. I was not an exception. I was trying to find answer to my own questions. Finding answers to one's own questions is very hard. Why did Minni feel that I am expecting something from our relationship? Did she think that I would be expecting physical relationship from her? Did she think that I would make her shunt Badri away from her and her children's thoughts? Did she imagine that I would expect her and the children to revolve around me.. and only around me? Many such questions began to rise in me one after the other. By the time I would answer one question another would pop up. I felt there were many more questions and these questions would keep coming up and I would have no control over them. If I should consider answering each of these was another question. When we do not find answers to some of our own questions at times it is better not to try finding answers to those. I did the same. I thought that I had successfully moved away from these questions. Suddenly another question popped up. "Am I not expecting anything from Minni? What is it that I am expecting?"

I struggled hard to find answers. I was totally helpless. I went back to Minni. It was quite early in the morning. Morning breeze was very inviting. We went for a long walk on the beachside. The ocean looked to be calm. But both of us were completely disturbed. There were violent waves troubling both of us from within. We were, apparently, very calm.

Now it was my turn. I started ...

ÞÞÞ

25

Chapter - 25

Minni, I don't think you are wrong in having a strong conviction that there cannot be any relationship without expectations. I always believe that relationships are to be nurtured. Some relationships are cherished. In the process of nurturing some relationships, relationships also get cherished. I am not here to claim that but for me there would not have been any one in this world for you and the children. You are the best example to understand that 'One needs none but oneself to live.' When one is completely with oneself, there will be many with one. But Minni, please understand all cannot be as strong as you are. You did not have a financially stable family, but I did. Badri had it. You enjoyed the passionate love of your mother. Badri had experienced some glimpses of it. I had a living mother..living father. They are still alive. But I never felt their love.. I never ever experienced it. To put it another way, I did not have father and mother in my life at all. Why..? Why it is so..? I don't know the answer. At times one may not get what one needs from things and people around one. I have never blamed my parents nor will I ever. Many envy my position. I know it is the highest position one can aspire. But in my journey till this day, I have traversed across many lives. I was close to many .. not so close to others. I was involved in the lives of some.. I myself voluntarily involved in the lives of a few others. I kept myself away from some.. All said and done, Minni, in all my relationship with others I always felt that I was obligated to do something. I was afraid of shirking away from my responsibilities, many of which were self -imposed. I stretched myself beyond my capabilities. There was always a relief of successful completion. But, if you ask me, whether I was satisfied ever, the answer is a clear 'NO'. We do many things for others. At times we do with their expectation and sometimes we do it out of our own liking without their expectation. And we do what we do in expectation of something in return. What is that something is completely individualistic. We feel lost when our expectations are not met. But we repeat the exercise of going behind someone or something else. The greatest tragedy of life is that every individual wants to be a hero to someone else other than to himself. You are, Minni, an exception. You took the entire responsibility of your life. You are completely in charge of your life. And, in the process, others came into your life. I appreciated you when you asked me to go away. You never got into a web. I am sure you will never be in a web. Nobody can even try to captivate you in a web. May be for the first time you are getting a feeling that you may get caught in my web. Aren't you feeling so, Minni? I asked her in a low voice looking straight into her eyes. She nodded her head in affirmation. I knew Minni would never lie. She would never ever lie to me. 'I promise you Minni, you will always remain free as you are now. You may remain the same with me as you have been without me. I have always included you in my life. It does not imply that you should also include me in your life. I want you to be a part of my life with all the assurance that you need not have me as a part of your life. This may look strange to you. I want to know what a Family is. I want to experience what it means to be in a Family. I want to be a part of a Family. I want to be a part of children's family ...of course if possible. I want myself to be a part of your Family. Minni, I beg you, please don't say "NO". I was unable to console myself. I was virtually begging .. I was begging for something which I needed. Which I had needed from the time I was a child. As I spoke to Minni I was looking down. Minni laid her hands on my shoulder. Then she lifted my chin slowly, looked deep into my eyes and said, "Come, let us go to the children." When someone looks so deep into your eyes, volumes are spoken. At times, a single seemingly disconnected sentence communicates a message which hundreds of words and lines do not. I got the answer to all my questions. I understood 'How foolish we are to expect life to give answers to all our questions in a particular manner. We design the questions. We try to design the answers as well. We expect answers to our questions in the same format in which we ask the questions. Why don't we understand that life has an altogether different mechanism to answer our questions? None of the questions in life go unanswered. We do get the answers. When, where and how, we can never tell.' I felt as though I got the answers. I moved.

I moved with Minni and the children. We decided to be together. The children were given to understand that our family would include me, Minni, Badri and the children. They were also very happy. The two elder children made it very clear that they would not call me dad. For them only Badri would be their Dad. I would only be RAY for them. I agreed. I knew for sure that I can never replace Badri in any body's life. I agreed for this commitment because I wanted to know what a father would mean to a child? I did not want to replace one father with another. Many letters addressed to the CM by many children had spoken to me as to what each child went through when it was asked to accept someone else as its mother or father than the one which the child wanted to accept or had already accepted. I did not want Badri and Minni's children to experience that agony. I decided that the children would continue to love Badri for ever. Even in his physical absence they would not miss out what a father would have done had he been physically present. Can I contribute a bit anywhere? If I can it is fine. If I cannot.. even then no issues. I will learn how the presence of a father in the life of a child, even for a very short period of the child's life, would bring a big difference in his/her upbringing.

26

Chapter - 26

Our life in a new city was too busy. Me, Minni, and the children were all too busy. We did not have a cook or a servant. I was in such a high position that I could get all these services. But we said 'No' and we decided to do all these by ourselves. Minni said the children should know the importance of every household chore and as they grow they should learn to respect labour in any of its forms. Minni started two non-profit organizations which looked into some of the concerns of children. I was too busy moving all over the world in connection with framing policies for the welfare of children. Doing household chores and attending to the needs and wants of the children was our best time. Often there would be fights between or amongst the siblings. We would watch silently, step in if necessary. When I spoke, Minni did not. When she said something, I never spoke against it. We both were constantly checking in our own way whether ours was a 'Family' for the children or not... The children went to a local school. They were considered as best. They were liked by all. All the three were different. The middle one was short tempered. It was surprising to see him losing his temper quite often, about anything which would matter least for others. The youngest one was very playful and wanted to live for the moment. He was not worried about anything. He loved to enjoy every little joy of life. It was a pleasure to see him being happy always. The eldest was always serious and of course thoughtful. Academics were not their forte for them except the eldest. At times there used to be comparisons. The three would pick up a quarrel or some outsider would have kindled the thought. Minni and I always showed them Badri's photo and told them, "Look, your father was a great lover of nature. Nature will not have single species. We are all different. But we are together. That is what a family means." I felt myself very lucky to find a family. I felt that my intrinsic worth was increasing and there was so much of value addition to me from every one in the family. I started realizing how minutely different we are from each other and distinguishable from each other. I arrived at a strong conclusion that the highest form of education can be received only from the family.

The children became very close to me. I repeatedly noticed that they were in deep love with me. I felt it. When someone loves you deeply you are bound to know it. You know it because you feel it. The power of feeling is amazingly strong. I also noticed that they were attached to me never being disrespectful to Minni. They looked up to me for everything... One night I noticed with my eyes closed the youngest getting into my room and covering me with the blanket that had slipped below the bed. The other day I found the middle one adjusting the lace of my shoes in perfect symmetry. I slowly started getting a feeling that I am now at the receiving end rather than being at the giving end. Again, the waves of questions started attacking me. Do the children love me because of my position? Do they love me because I do everything for them and their mother which I was not obliged to? Are they feeling obligated to me? Am I misinterpreting their obligation to me as love? In the innermost corner of my heart I had no guts to even whisper to myself that the children did not love me. My only anxiety was, "whether it was in return for something?" All said and done I was sure of one thing. I did not want the children to get a wrong message as to what love is.

If I were to define love as something people would invest only to get something in return, I could say that I was getting the best returns on my investment. But that was not my definition of love.

Suddenly another question popped up. What did Badri get from his relationship with Minni and the children? This question was bugging me too much. Minni was worried because I was worried. She asked me ... 'Ray .something is bothering you. Can you share it with me? Being hesitant, I postponed it initially. I later got convinced that if I did not share with Minni what was troubling me, it would be dishonesty on my part. I told her, 'Minni, I wanted to know what Badri got from his relationship with you?' Minni was surprised by my question. Her answer was profound. 'Ray, what one gets from one's relationship with another is unique. Do you think you can get what Badri got or did not get?' She moved towards the locker. Removing all the valuable things stored there she took out a neatly packed parcel. I noticed that she was in a confused state. She slowly said, 'Ray, I had received this parcel in the morning of the same day on which Badri died. I did not open it. I had just put it as it was received. Badri had told me that he was working with a famous artist to get our family portrait painted. I was expecting the artist to come and make us all sit and draw and paint our pictures. It never happened. When I asked Badri about it, he said, 'This is an altogether different type of portrait. The artist will see everyone in front of his eyes, but no one sits before the artist.' Knowing Badri as a weird person, I did not dig too much into it. Today, when you asked me what Badri got from his relationship with me. I was surprised because this same question had haunted me even when Badri was alive. Honestly speaking I do not have an answer to it. However, for the first time, I felt that I should open the parcel sent by the artist.

We both sat together and opened the parcel carefully. Before we could open the frame, there was a brief letter by the artist addressed to Badri. 'Mr. Baddyson, thank you so much for giving me an opportunity to draw the portrait of your wonderful family. Each member of your family is unique. Together you are all amazing. Remember, I had told you before I took up the assignment, that, if I do not catch the character of each of the members of your family in this portrait, as depicted by you, then get me back to those persons, I will work on it again. I stand by my words. Looking forward to hearing from you if such need arises.'

We opened the strong cover .. the picture was awesome. We both felt that we are all in the picture together. There were- a big tree... small plants, a lady, a man- another man ..three small children ...a butterfly.. two women peeping from the sky. I asked Minni to identify each one there. We both took two slips and wrote down who were all there. Both the slips matched precisely. We both understood, the lady in the picture to be Minni, the two men to be Badri and me. And the three little children. Two women peeping from the sky were Minni's mother and Badri's mother and the butterfly was my favourite. We could not decipher what the tree in the picture meant.

Surprisingly there was a line written above the picture in Badri's hand over that read, "Family has everything that nature has." As per the wish of Badri we both decided to place the picture in the living room.

Every time I looked at the picture I wanted to know why the 'tree' was there. I knew somewhere in the deepest corner of my heart that I also wanted to know more about Badri. Day by day Badri had become a puzzle to me. Have I failed to understand Badri? Or, have I understood him as he was required to be understood? I was unable to accept my defeat. Being unable to handle my restlessness I went to meet James, the artist.

ÞÞÞ

27

Chapter - 27

I had done my own research from several quarters about Artist James. None called him a weird person but those who had acquaintance with him said he was a peculiar person. He always dictated his terms first and then to listen to others' terms if any. As I sought his appointment, his secretary sent a note which just read, "Listen to me, if you want to be listened to." I had absolutely no objection. I always loved listening. I felt very happy to listen to an artist chosen and trusted by Badri. His secretary asked me whether it would be alright with me to meet James at his home rather than at his studio. I agreed.

James came out to receive me. It was a small house but amazingly clean. There was complete calmness. Within minutes I could get to understand that James was a minimalist. He did not speak much. When I told him the purpose of my visit, he stared at me for a while. Suddenly he went out leaving me all alone there. Came back after fifteen to twenty minutes and asked me, "Mr. Reon, have you come here to understand more about the picture or about Baddyson?" I did not want to lie. I replied in a confessing tone , 'The picture on the one hand and of course more about Baddyson, on the other.' James said, 'Mr.Reon, I don't know much about Baddyson. All I know about him is through the picture. Even after knowing completely well as to what you are, and how big a position you hold, I am compelled by myself to be blunt with you. I am sorry to know that you could not understand Baddyson through the picture. I am equally sorry to know that people like you who claim to be working for children do not understand the language of silence. I am surprised that you are unable to decipher what is not said in words, which according to me would be the basic qualification to understand children.' I did not get angry. I looked at James. He understood that I was being apologetic.

'Ok. Mr.Reon, do you want to see my Family's picture?' He took me to his bed room. There was the picture of a mirror with a carved frame. The frame had several parts with asymmetrical designs painted in totally unmatching rather mismatching colours. The painting of the mirror looked so natural that I thought he had fixed a real mirror there, and had painted only the frame. I was surprised. When I started appreciating his skill, he stopped me in between. 'Mr. Reon, I have reached a position in life where I don't need appreciation. I want understanding. The mirror is my family. Whenever I see myself I see the entire family, I don't see myself alone. For me one cannot be beyond one's family. Mr.Reon, you being at the helm of affairs, should see to it that a child does not miss the family at any cost. This world is too large. The world is too large not to get the family for every child. I respect Baddyson because he knew how important the 'family' is for a child, for every child. Now, answering your question, 'Mr.Reon, the big tree in the picture is the 'FAMILY '. It is there standing so big, standing so strong and huge. Unfortunately, it is not understood. At times it is misunderstood.'

James continued..

'Mr.Reon, I state my own terms when someone approaches me to draw a family picture. I have heard some complaining about it. Many who had agreed initially, moved away half way through, even at the cost of losing the initial deposit of fifty percent of my huge bills. I tell them to talk uninterruptedly for two hours per day continually for ten days. One should speak about everything one has gone through in life and every person whom one considers important and why. I have always respected self-talk. Talking about yourself to yourself is a cleansing process. It is a wonderful solo-journey. Unfortunately, we don't have others' eyes and hearts and touch to listen to us in this world. We feel stressed.. we feel lost because we are either misunderstood or not understood. I ask my customers to go through this process because I want to understand whether they have understood themselves or not. Some are hesitant to talk. I ask them to write down. Many prefer this. As days move, I indicate to them to work on how many can be removed from the picture . This is to make the picture easier and understandable . If you see my family picture I see only myself if I see in the mirror. But if both of us see simultaneously in the mirror, you are also there. But only at that particular point of time. Not for ever. At times, I myself am not there. Mr. Reon, I may sound philosophical but I tell you, 'ultimately we are all , each one of us is, single in this world. We come across each other accidentally.. and we move away from one another ....'. But with all this I tell you 'family' is something which holds us all together. In my picture, there is a frame. In the frame there are so many designs, random colours. They are all outsiders. But the picture cannot stand alone without the frame. The frame is not the picture. Nevertheless, it gives strength to the picture. In Baddyson's picture it is the tree. It is very rare to see persons like Baddyson in this world. Look at who are all included in the picture of his family. That is what drew me nearer to Baddyson.

Do you know, within seven days after a family picture drawn by me is received, the person concerned should come back and receive the video recordings or the written notes from me. I assure them of confidentiality. Now that Baddyson is no more, I can handover what was written by him to you and Minni. Otherwise I will destroy it.'

I went to artist Jame's house with a prior appointment along with Minni. James handed over the file to me. He said in his deep stern voice, "I don't think Mr. Baddyson will ever die." Hearing this, Minni and I looked at each other. Did James understand Baddyson better than either of us...?

ꝑꝑꝑ

28

Chapter - 28

Here goes what Badri had written ...

Mr.James,

You wanted me to speak.. I could not..I cannot.. I feel that when thoughts get converted into spoken words the sound intervenes.. I have chosen the subtler version. I have chosen to write. I request you to listen to my inner voice. Eliminate the unwanted sounds. Eliminate everything that is a waste. You being a minimalist, I am sure, you would handle it well.

I am getting an intuition that I will not live long.

However you may take your own time..

Trusting you..

Baddyson...

29

Chapter - 29

This is what Badri had written..

I do not know where to start with. I never knew that writing would be so difficult. That too when it comes to writing about yourself. It does not mean writing a story. I cannot imagine things. I have to state the truth, nothing but the truth ..as they say in courts. Let me begin it from my mother. What a beautiful human being she was! What a comfort it was to stand, sit and sleep next to her. How good I used to feel to squeak into her blanket. I still feel her smell. It was unique. I tried to get it from different people. None smelled like her. I remember how she would try with great difficulty to move from the bed to lift me as I would run away from servants and would run to her to get on to her bed. What a bright smile it was. I could see the brightness in her eyes getting brighter even with the tears. That is something strange I could not understand as a child. That is the brightness one can see in a mother's eyes through which she sees her child. Each of the three servants at our big bungalow would attend to me. I have heard them saying Badi Deediji /my mother is an angel, she has never hurt anyone in her life. She is all into giving. Ten years into marriage she did everything to please my father and his relatives who remained true to themselves by being unsatisfied with my mother all the while. My mother prayed every God and did everything that everyone advised her to do to get a child. As time was running fast, everyone decided that my father should get married again. My mother did not oppose. She knew she had none to listen to her. It was at that time Chotiji entered my father's life as his second wife. My mother's trouble increased multifold day by day. Chotiji was all powerful and dominant. I have heard maids' gossips about her. Chotiji did not have her character straight. She had an affair with her own brother-in-law. To put a full stop to all these, she was given in marriage to my father. She brought with her fortune in abundance adding to what my greedy father already had. Everyone and everything was being controlled by her. The equations did not go as per everyone's calculations. My mother got pregnant. Chotiji did not. I was born. Chotiji did not have any children. Chotiji started her open war against me and my mother. My mother who was strong and healthy, began to get weaker and became helpless when Chotiji's attack was on me. She would touch me and pray God "Oh God, save this child from Choti." My father was a mute spectator. The maids called him spineless. I have heard many a time what Choti would tell my father, 'You are not a man at all. I know, may be your first wife.. that.. "XXX" has slept with someone and given birth to this "xxxx".' She would point fingers at me. My mother became very sick. She was unable to move. She was totally bedridden. I heard from the gossip of the maids that Chotiji had used black magic on my mother and she mixed something in milk and fed my mother, every day , stealthily , which made her paralytic. How much of trauma I was going through no one understood. I was not even allowed to go near my own mother. Choti had instructed everyone to see to it that my mother did not get a chance even to see me. The maids were kind to me. They understood what a child needs and what a mother would die to get. With their help I could steal time to get a chance to run into her room, touch her, lick her cheeks and get a small weak hug from her. But the strength I would get from her hugs was unique. I have never felt strengthened by anything else in this world. None can give what a mother can. I could see the fear in my mother's eyes whenever I approached her. Her eyes would always be on the door. Many a time, Chotiji came like a devil, snatched me and hit me with whatever was in her hand and threatened me with dire consequences if ever I went near my mother. She would pick a fierce fight with the maids and hold a big enquiry as to who allowed me inside my mother's room. I still remember the Diwali festival days, when all had to go to the temple. Chotiji would kiss me before all the society people pretending to be the best mother ever for me. She thought I, being a child, would not recognise her other face. She did not know the power of a child's comprehension. What a child understands as a child is amazing. No one can understand it better. But unfortunately a child cannot express what it actually understands, and there is no one in this world to understand the understanding of a child. Child's language is completely child-specific. Seven years was too much.. I understood everything. Circumstances make you understand the situation fast. One day I had hidden myself behind the long drawn very thick window curtains as I saw Choti getting into my mother's room.

By then the maid had already placed the milk glass on the side table and gone out. After the maid left, Choti closed the door. I saw her mixing some black powder in my mother's milk. She forced it into my mother's mouth. My mother's resistance was unbearable for me to withstand. I remembered what maids had gossiped amongst themselves secretly that Chotiji would give some black magic medicine to my mother so that my mother would stop talking also and would become weak day by day and would forget to recognise anyone and would forget to eat and gulp to die eventually one day.

I don't know what came over me. I came out, pulled the side table and struck Choti on her head with all force. She had a big bandage over her head. She avoided coming in front of me. The maids told me that Choti was afraid of me. Many gave me multiple suggestions. I sat in front of them. They thought I was listening to them. No one knew that I was listening to something else. I was listening to the agony my mother went through. I was listening to what all she was talking to me silently. I was repeatedly listening to the gossip of the maids. I was listening to all the advice she would give me in a half minute's meeting with me.

I trusted the maids. My mother was becoming weaker day by day. She had ceased to speak. She would not recognise me immediately. One day I was told that my mother died. I remember the previous night when I went near her, she lifted her hand with difficulty and pointed it upwards. May be she showed that there is God to take care. That is the last I can remember about my mother. Now I understand when one is sure that no one around can help, one would look up to someone who is not there, who is not visible. My mother was no different. Perhaps, she thought there was GOD over there to protect me. Mr James, as I am writing this I am feeling as though God is watching me. God is watching me that I have not forgotten my mother. My sweet mother, the sweetest human being I have ever had in my life.

A year after my mother's death there was a ceremony arranged at home. After that Choti decided that she would sleep on the bed where my mother was sleeping. I did not want it to happen. I knew my father would not oppose it because he had surrendered to Choti's money. Her power of wealth had controlled everyone including my father. As all were discussing Choti's move into my mother's room and sleeping on the bed with my father, no one bothered to ask me about my opinion. When I entered the room Choti shouted at me. Her bitter and obscene, below the belt language was piercing enough to make any one run away. But she did not know the power of words. She did not know how they would pounce on her. By then I had brought a big strong piece of wood kept in our traditional bath room to be used to heat water. I don't know from where I mustered the strength, I once again struck Choti on her head. One does not know the strength a child gets, when someone tries to encroach its personal space and invade and cause serious damage to the ones the child feels obligated to protect, for the reasons best known to the child. For me my mother was everything. For me my mother was still alive. I did not want her place to be usurped by anyone, far less by Choti.

Everything to follow was quite expected. Choti influenced my father to send me away and get me behind the bars. When my father hesitated, not because he was not willing, but was afraid that the entire society would speak ill of him, Choti lodged the complaint herself. The police took me .. they enquired about me.. came to my school also. I know it was Reon who saved me. I know it was our Principal who understood me.

30

Chapter - 30

Mr. James, I should tell you something about Reon. But for Reon I would have been nowhere in this world. What an influence a childhood friend can have on one even when he grows into an adult individual is something unique. I still remember the occasion I met Reon. I was standing in the queue with my father when Reon came to school to get admitted. I was waiting there to pay the school fees. I was already a senior. I had failed in class 1 twice, as half the year I had remained absent. As I stood in the queue, I watched everything that went between Reon's father and mother. I knew how Reon was named as Reon. All through I was silently watching Reon. His focus was on the butterfly which was trying hard to move out of the closed window. I remember even to this day how Reon came back, trying hard to get through the crowd in the Principal's chamber, climbed over the table and moved past the Principal and bent over and opened the strong window only to liberate that struggling butterfly. In retrospect, I feel how strong Reon's conviction was. He was not afraid of anyone. He did what he felt to be right. He did not find himself to be answerable to anyone. This first impression was something that drew me nearer to

Reon. That day, I found there was something special and unique in him. Now I understand, he was focussed. He had clarity of thought. He did not bother about anything else. He always pursued what was important and never broke his head on unimportant issues.

We spoke very little to each other. But every time I did something he, appreciated me, either through a single word or through gestures. When I said something about our drawing teacher's stinking mouth everyone looked at me as though I committed a crime. When I asked Reon whether I did something wrong, he told me, "It requires strength to utter the truth knowing fully well that you are in a vulnerable position." When I helped him secure the butterflies from out of the squeezing hands of Sandeep, by giving reply justifying my actions, I saw a deep sense of appreciation in Reon's eyes. I am yet to find such sincere appreciation in this world. Minni has expressed her gratitude but if I can recollect what would be true appreciation, I would say , it is the one I got from and only from Reon. I have heard people say that you need a family where you get all the nourishments and I know appreciation is the most required nutrition for a child. Who can give it to a child other than a family member? Reon has always been a member of my family. Unfortunately, people fail to understand who the members of the family of a child are. Till death, what the child has conceptualised as a family will continue to be with the child. A child's family cannot be substituted or replaced by anyone. Unfortunately, everyone fails to understand what it is that constitutes a family for every child? A child's search to include many others in its family may continue as it grows into an adult and beyond.

How important was Minni for Reon was something that drew me closer to Reon. I loved Reon not because I could share something with him but because he could share many things with me which, for sure, he had never shared with anyone else. We love people with whom we share and open up ourselves. I loved Minni because of that particular connecting thread between me and her. I loved Reon because he shared everything with me. That was a special connecting thread. I saw my mother in him. Unfortunately, my mother also had many things to communicate to me, but could not. She might have thought that I was unable to understand her. She did not know that I understood every situation she did not speak about and every word that did not come from her mouth. The same was the situation with Reon. I understood his weakness. Reon could not transform thoughts into words. Reon was a doer. May be, I learnt the art of listening to what is not being articulated, from my mother.

It is true that I was disappointed too much as I noticed that I was not there in the drawing of Reon's family. Yet I consoled myself. I understood that he wanted me more to listen to him, to be with him but he had some others. At that age itself I could understand that for me he was more important. I love him, that is important for him, and that is important for me too. I did not give up the hope that 'one day Reon would also love me.' But I was sure of one thing. Even if Reon's family may not have me, Reon would definitely be there if I have a family any day.

Things were going too hostile for me to handle them as a child. I had someone called 'Father' who was completely emotionless and callous towards me. Then there was Choti charged with wild emotions against me, the maid servants wanting to help me but were unable to.. my mother's vacant bed everyday was inviting me but was strangely kicking me strongly when I went near it ... All these became too trying for me - too much of a load for a child. There was none to take it off me. The school was attractive to me because of Reon and the Principal. There were others too. There were expectations from every child of the school including me. I was the one who could not be tied by others' expectations. I failed everyone but not Reon and the Principal because, they did not express any of their expectations to me. I thought I should understand their expectations and fulfil them. The police coming often to the school, people coming from juvenile justice committee, having repeated meetings at school and the Principal trying to save me at every stage were becoming too cumbersome for me. The worst of the humiliations suffered by me in life was when Choti came to school with a bandage wrapped around her head completely and standing alongside the teachers when the prayer was going on. She wanted to make it visible to everyone as to how I had hit her . Her bandage was disproportionate to the wound she had suffered. Her continued stay in the school, sitting right in front of the Principal and forcing him to get me to him and talking to me in her presence, was too taxing for me. I knew how embarrassing it would have been for the Principal. I knew how the Principal had tried his best to postpone the action. But the Principal failed before Choti's power. He asked the P.T. Master to get me to his chambers. I knew for sure it was all to face Choti the Great. I came running with the dumbbells in my hand. As Choti started making accusations against me I was trying to keep myself under control. The moment Choti started uttering four letter words against my mother, nothing could contain me. I hit Choti left and right with the dumb-bells in my hand, the Principal intervened, and, Choti ran out of the school to save herself. After she left, the Principal did not speak to me. He just laid his hands on my shoulders, poured a glass of water from his personal water bottle, asked me to sip and drink. I did. After a few minutes, he said, 'You may go.' At that moment I knew how one can understand another without the help of words. Our Principal could sense how a child would feel if his mother is humiliated and ill-treated. That is why he did not beat me ..did not even scold me. However, I firmly decided to quit and move out. The day on which I wanted to move out, I went sheepishly inside the Principal's chamber. I told him, "Sir, I am going." The Principal held my shoulders fast looking deep into my eyes for a minute. I saw tears and also a sparkle in his eyes. It was very much the same as the ones I had seen in my mother's eyes. He just said, "You will WIN. Wait for that day". Leaving me there he went out. I then wrote letter to Reon and gave it to an ayah and asked her to give it to Reon and walked out of the school gate discarding my bag near the gate.

I don't know how I reached the railway station....how many trains I changed. I picked and ate whatever was being thrown away by passengers. No one caught me travelling ticketless because everyone thought I was with some adult who was travelling by the train. I reached a place of pilgrimage. Any journey has to conclude at some point or the other. I got down there. I went to two or three shops seeking a job but could not get one.

But people were good. Some gave me food, some gave me tea, some offered me chocolates, biscuits, banana and water. While sitting on a stone bench near the bus stand with a strong conviction to face life all alone I saw an elderly man or Kakku struggling hard to carry three or four heavy bags with him. I ran to him and offered to help. I carried his bags to his big shop. When he tried to pay me, I said, "I don't want to accept it Sir, as that was not the contract between us." He felt moved. He offered me a job. My good command over English and Hindi made his business boom. I attracted customers. I was well built, at eleven - twelve I looked like a sixteen year old. Kakku increased my salary, started giving me cuts when I brought some provisions from villagers and made him gain profit. All my expenses were met by Kakku. As money got accumulated, the thought of Reon and Minni began to haunt me. I went to every construction site, waited for hours and came back home with an empty heart. Gradually, I began to lend money to labourers and earn interest and then I started lending money to masons and contractors. Money multiplied very soon. I left Kakku with a happy note. I started my finance company. I knew that it was a bloody business for people like me. I had to grow strong. My network with people with no moral frames also continued. I had decided that money for me was either paper or steel and I wanted more in exchange. I did not bother who borrowed it for what purpose. I hoped I would slowly rise on the ladder of life. I was not even aware when everyone who were supposed to be with me left me. But money did not leave me. My growth was amazingly sudden and straight. I had everything a very rich person could claim to possess. Many women came into my life. I did not have any attachment to anyone. It was just body for body and body for money(?). I understood what sex is but did not understand what was meant by physical relationship. Many forced me to get married. I refused. I thought I would get married only if I was confident that I would gain a family through that person. Only when I was confident that I could have a family will I go for marriage with that person that very day. No one fulfilled my parameters. I was growing older. My search for Minni and Reon also continued.

31

Chapter - 31

Mr. James, the contractor knew about my craze after women. He knew how I would pour money and go behind one and get back in hours with frustration in my eyes. He claimed that he understood what I wanted. He introduced me to a lady. He said she was different. 'You will see womanhood in her. You will discover completeness in her. You may find peace by being with her. You may get disturbed too.' That is how I was brought to that lady. The elegance, grace and the composed demeanour of that lady strummed my chord directly. The voice was low and slow but, firm. She looked as though she knew and had understood the whole world and it would not be difficult for her to understand me. My need for understanding was understood by her is what I felt in our first meeting. However, I failed in my attempt at playing with her body. Forget about sex, I could not even touch her properly. Something in her was repelling me from going near her.

Days and months passed by. Everyday, I would go to her and return incomplete. There was some vacuum which stood as a wall between us. One day I drank heavily and decided that 'it should be today ..and today at any cost'. But as I started removing her dress down the shoulders, I saw the butterfly tattoo on her shoulder. I was startled. I found that she was Reon's Minni. I realised why I was unable to look at her body from the perspective with which I had played with other women.

I put her dress back. Brought her gently out of the bed. I held her hand and led her to our portico. We sat and talked for hours. Her narrative of her life was touching. I could see a complete woman in her. Growing from dust she had risen to different levels, met with several hard challenges but had never lost hopes in life. She had no complaints against the world. She was filled with zeal. She was prepared to spread that message of the ever living spirit of life wherever she went. She spread it to all those who ever came across her. The fact that she gave birth to three children was something too striking to understand her inner strength. The fact that she decided to choose and fix on a single partner for the sake of her three children was more striking. What does Minni want in this relationship with me? I questioned myself. She had enough money, her own money. I thought I was the real beneficiary. I thought it was the best opportunity for me to understand completeness. I extended my hands to her.

The paperwork was done quickly. I became Minni's husband officially. I maintained a healthy distance from her physically. I noticed that Minni was disturbed. There were some questions troubling her from within that I wanted to address but went on postponing. My frequent business trips to different countries held me.

One day my meeting with another business tycoon got cancelled. I cut short my trip of ten days and came back home on the second day itself. I saw a note on Minni's bed that said, 'she was getting a plastic surgery done to remove the butterfly tattoo from her shoulder.' I felt I was deceived. I rushed to the hospital and brought her back home. I wanted the butterfly to stay on her shoulder. I had quixotic thoughts running through my mind. Is Minni being disloyal to Reon after all these years? This was unacceptable to me. Or is it that.. she was trying to be loyal to me and the butterfly was coming in her way? I did not talk to Minni for a whole week. There was no silence between us..but there was stone walling. There were so many soundless words moving between us which did not give any meaning to either of us. It was a suffocating experience for both of us. Even the children sensed the smell.

Minni took the initiative. She entered my room and asked me reasons for keeping myself away from her. Why was I hesitant? She reminded me as to how many times she came near me and it was I who always said "NO". She was sobbing. I went with her. Slowly I made her sit on the bed. I started crying. I cried so much for the first time. I was troubled that I had been misunderstood by her. I opened up. I explained to her, 'Minni, don't feel obligated to me. That pains me a lot. You are not obligated to me in any way. Don't ever feel that you are doing injustice to me by not sleeping naked next to me. Please understand that the relationship between me and you is far above that. But I know, know for sure that you belong to Reon. I can only protect you. Nothing beyond.. I have promised Reon that I will get you back to him. What I am getting from my relationship with you is known only to me. Today I have a perfect family. I now know what a mother is..what she does..I now know what children are..how they are part of ourselves and our thoughts emotions and feelings. I now know how they get connected to us..and how they get connected to the world through us.. I now know what a home is.. It is all because of you Minni.. I am more indebted to you than you suppose you are to me. Do not feel obligated. Love does not flourish under the roof of obligation. No one should be obligated to love or demonstrate love for others. Love is beyond obligation. It is beyond demonstration. Love can be felt. It is something which has to be believed. I love you. I love you for what you are. Next to my mother I don't think I loved anyone else in this world. I don't think I love Reon too. May be Yess or may be No. I am not sure on this. But I am sure I loved my mother and I love you. I am equally sure that I feel obligated to Reon. The day on which I see you meet Reon I would feel fulfilment.

I started my search for Reon amidst my busy schedule. May be I could have done it long ago. My high level contacts could have helped me. But why I did not try is something strange. It is not as though I never thought of Reon at all. In fact, many a time Reon came in my thoughts. Minni was not much there. When there was a soothing breeze I remembered my mother. When there was a straight focussed decision from my end, I remembered Reon. Memories of both my mother and Reon had a soothing effect on me. No one can imagine what childhood can yield. The treasures of childhood is unique to each child. Going through almost the mid -age of my life I still cherish those treasures. I value them the most. Could anyone other than me even guess what is in my treasure island? Everyone simply tries to meddle with children's lives. No one understands that there are secret nooks in every child's heart where no one can ever peep even for a fraction of a second. No one can ever understand that child remains alive till the death of an individual.

Probably, as I found Minni my wish for finding and meeting Reon became stronger and stronger within me. At times a true sense of obligation makes one more focussed. I started searching for Reon ..

Soon I found out that Reon is a big man. He is big in a real sense. I wondered what I would be. I thought of the picture I had drawn for him. Me holding him on my shoulders. After knowing every bit about Reon I thought, may be today, if I was asked to draw the picture I would be on his shoulders. A lot of material was available on the internet about Reon. Every action and every word of Reon had value. I gradually understood.. Reon was trying to see Minni, me and himself in every child. He had understood what all the three of us had missed as children. He understood what every child should not be missing. He was struggling hard to bridge the gap wherever children missed what they should not be missing. His Mission "Family for the Children" was something that shook my nerves. I thought, perhaps, if Reon is asked to draw the picture again, I would definitely be there.

Reon's another Mission, "I am here to listen to you".. was very popular. Any child could dial the numbers, speak for any length of time. There would be patient, empathetic listening from the other end. There would be no intervention, no preaching, no advice. Just listening. Children were not judged. No opinions were formed. They were not given any suggestions. They were listened to. Deeply.. with a commitment to understand that child. I was told that many adolescents who had thought of ending their lives were saved by such an initiative. I was told that Reon himself would find time amidst his busy schedule to listen to at least 2-3 children every day .

'The World is too Big', another mission of Reon, helped adults suffering from the traces of childhood abuse and trauma to overcome the same. It had multiple projects to show the depressed that the world is sufficiently large to find happiness and comfort and when one is blessed with abundance one need not crib on what he/she missed out as a child.

There were volunteers from every corner of the world. I felt proud of myself. I was happy that Reon was my classmate and I was his. Reon is a living example as to how effectively one can mould oneself and mould the lives of others notwithstanding the disadvantageous position in which one is stuck with.

I just started reflecting. What more would I need? I suddenly remembered what our Principal had said on the day when I decided to move out of the school and my city, " You will win. Wait for that Day." I now know that I have Won. I have Won. There remains nothing more to Win. I am successful. I feel complete. I know I can reach out to Reon within no time.

While I decided that meeting Reon was my first priority, somehow I began to get a stronger gut feeling that I may not be able to live with him. I don't know why this thought began to recur in mind frequently. I did not share it with Minni either. I somehow felt Reon and I may not be able to sit next to each any more to talk about Minni or butterflies..or my mother. I felt I could only go near Reon but I will not be able to talk to him..hug him. I strongly felt once again that I would not get that hug from Reon which would remind me of my mother's hug. My intuition was repeatedly bringing such thoughts to me.

Mr James, as these thoughts repeatedly came to my mind as though they were serious pieces of warning, I decided to go for a Family Portrait. Keeping aside the project of meeting Reon, I first decided to meet you Mr. James, and go ahead with getting the portrait done. I have already spoken to you for some time about our background. I wanted you to have these details too. I think by now you would have understood who all and what all should be there in our family portrait.

Eagerly waiting to see the portrait.

Thank you, Mr. James.

Baddyson.

32

Chapter - 32

The letter written by Badri to Artist James was much more than a mere letter. For me it was the unlocking of a child from prison. His letter made me understand that every part of life has its own significance and has a strong impact on the other part. Unfortunately, we try to disassociate ourselves from the parts and try to handle each part individually. Probably that is where we escape from reaching completion. Badri knew the true meaning of completion in human life. Badri knew for sure what fulfilment in life was. He lived for it. He was struggling hard to keep all the parts together. It was evident. His struggle yielded him the true success he deserved. Badri had evolved himself as a complete man in the process. He could achieve it because he had surrendered himself to the process of living. He was not an escapist. He wanted to meet life as it is. He loved life as it is. I got confirmed that whether we like it or not, every part of our life is interwoven with the other. However, one that is suppressed and put down below would pop up and disturb the other parts. Childhood being the foundational part it can render the other parts of life topsy turvy or make them stronger too.

I understood his letter and the portrait in my own way. And Minni understood it differently. Tears started rolling from her eyes. She went near the portrait. Looked at it deeply. I could feel that the family portrait was speaking to her and she was into deeply reflective listening from her side. She gave herself away to understand the Family Portrait exhaustively and through it to understand Badri completely.

Children came from somewhere all of a sudden. Each was excited to see the big family portrait. Each started looking at something. Each wanted to find where Badri was in that portrait. I could gather from their discussion that for them Badri was the hero. What a wonderful father Badri was for the children. I understood. For a moment me and Minni understood and felt how the love of father would be. How important is father for a child. Badri was a complete father for the children.

ÞÞÞ

33

Chapter - 33

YESSSSSS

Everything happened as Badri had thought. He and I could not live together. His intuition was right. From where he got the intuition that he would not be there for long I don't know.

I received a telegraphic message one day from my secretary that someone from my hometown would like to meet me to give me a surprise. In spite of repeated requests he has not been revealing his identity., and that he is hell bent upon meeting me. For a minute I tried guessing who he could be ..then ...I left it in between. I gave the appointment. It was at 4 P.M. I parked my car and was crossing the road. I was in my own world. I did not bother to watch the signal. A big truck was rushing from one side. I remember having seen it. I could have gone back..some how I continued. Suddenly a car came from another side. Before the truck could hit me, it hit the car. Everything happened in a fraction of a second. I just fell down in shock.

There was so much of commotion. The car had literally turned into scrap. And the only one in the car who was driving the car had died on the spot. The police came and they recognised me through my ID Card. Someone was telling the other onlooker that the car driver saved me and he died in the process. I stood there till the end. I was shocked to know that the driver was Baddyson who was supposed to meet me. The documents with him, the phone call records, the messages revealed that he had a family. The body was kept in the mortuary. His family arrived. I was a mute spectator. I met Minni and the three children in the mortuary. I broke down, Minni also broke down. She broke down more because Badri had moved away from this world without meeting me. She was mature enough to accept the fact of his death. She was irreconcilable because Badri's wish to meet me had remained unfulfilled. The children were shattered. What the death of a father would mean to children is something which cannot be explained in words. Badri had donated his body. There was nothing much to be done. We moved out. Half way through, suddenly Minni held my hand and asked if we go to Badri once again. Considering my position, the authorities obliged. We both went there. Minni held my hand and put our both hands on the heart of Badri. She said, 'Ray, listen to him.. listen to what he says. He is telling something. Others thought she was speaking being in a shock. But I understood .. I understood her completely. I understood what she was trying to express. It was true. Badri spoke to both of us. Separately and together. We both listened. Separately and collectively. What a dead man communicates to the living and how he would do, can only be experienced. I was surprised to know that even the dead speak. Slowly we both looked at each other. Then we both declared Badri as finally physically DEAD. Came out, ..without Badri?..No ... yet with Badri. We both knew that Badri would always live with us.

34

Chapter - 34

The children got into liking me gradually. But I could sense clearly that they never wanted me to take the place of Badri. I was strongly hit when the eldest once told me in a harsh voice, 'Don't ever try to pretend to be our father. You can never be him.. however big you may be.. however a great hero you may be to the whole world. For us, only he is our hero..' He fingered at the large portrait of Badri. It sounded like a stern warning. But I took it as a strong message to me. I understood for the first time that children do not like replacements. They want the originals. As a child who I did not have? Whom I did not want to be replaced..and why? I knew the answer. Who was never acceptable to Badri to be replaced in his life and why? Whom Minni did not want to be replaced and why? I started reflecting. We, the three of us, resisted the same thing. We kept on resisting in our own way throughout. I understood that when children resist we should not feel bad about it. I started empathising with the children. I always placed Badri first. I convinced them and impressed on them that I had no intention of replacing their father. I made them slowly understand how Badri was a real hero for me too.

Minni felt a little bit disturbed whenever the children revolted against me. Over a period of time, we both decided to explain to the children everything about our journey of life. We felt they were old enough to understand. We told them to take a decision of their own. I made it clear to them that I would be there in their lives as long as they wanted me to be there. How would I tell them all this? I wrote this book, I am Reon. Minni went through it. She edited it here and there and she said, 'It is now ripe for children to read'. We made three copies of it and gave it to each one of them.

Minni and I were extremely happy that we had not hidden anything from the children. We wanted to be transparent. We wanted them to respect and encourage transparency in their lives. We knew that they might get disturbed but thought that they should know how to handle it. It becomes too difficult for parents to be transparent with their children. But transparency connects individuals at a deeper level. Connections and deeper understanding amongst me, Badri and Minni could happen only because there was transparency in our relationship and we respected each other's space. We accepted each other gracefully without being judgmental. We wanted the same to be passed on to our children too.

The children read the book. Perhaps, they cried. May be, they were angry..may be, they were disturbed. But the end result was that they all came to Minni and me, as we both were drinking our evening tea sitting in the balcony overlooking the beach. The eldest said, 'We wanted to tell you both our conclusions after reading the book.' We both looked at them. Despite being fifty plus we were both shivering within. We were afraid of listening to something which may not be acceptable from our perspective. How strange we human beings are! We even decide what we want to listen to even before the other chooses to speak to us. Minni gesticulated to them to go ahead. They all said in a single voice, “Life is Beautiful. We want to live it to the fullest.”

Minni hugged me. Tears began to roll down my cheeks too. Minni started licking those tears..very slowly.. unmindful of the children’s presence.. I felt the butterflies were there on my cheeks. I found my two butterflies back. I felt extremely happy and complete.

ÞÞÞ

QUESTIONS????????????

After I completed writing this short novel I still have this question haunting me ..

Who is the Hero figure in this novel?

Badri? Reon? Minni? Minni's Mom? Children?

Or

The Butterflies?

S.SUSHEELA.

www.ingramcontent.com/pod-product-compliance
Lightning Source LLC
LaVergne TN
LVHW091330150826
845673LV00006B/1817

* 9 7 9 8 8 9 3 2 2 7 8 0 2 *